"Jocelyn," he said softly. "I fell in love with you that very day I first saw you. I fell in love with a stranger, a beautiful girl with dark hair and grey eyes who would not tell me her name." He took her face between his hands. "I wanted to kiss you. But you were afraid. Are you still afraid?"

She put her arms around his neck and responded to the touch of his lips with all the passion she had stiffled for so long. Then almost roughly she freed herself from his arms. She lifted her hands to her flushed cheeks. What madness seized her, to let Adam make love to her, and to reveal her own feelings to him. She knew what she must do. She must tell him swiftly and honestly, that it was useless, his waiting for her to be free. But she knew if she told him the truth the love in his eyes would change to scorn as he realized that she had cheated him.

Sobbing she ran away from him down the path. She couldn't bear to do it, she couldn't. Through the shame and distress of her tortured mind she heard his voice call after her.

"Jocelyn my love, come back. What is it? What have I done to you, don't run away..."

Also by the author: *

HOUSE OF GRANITE
THE GENEROUS VINE
IF THIS BE LOVE
PRELUDE TO LOVE
THE SPANISH DOLL
VALLEY OF NIGHTINGALES
WOMAN FROM THE SEA

* Available in ACE STAR Editions

ELIZABETH RENIER

1st Prize Winner, Romantic Novelists Assoc.

VALLEY
OF SECRETS

ACE BOOKS

A Division of Charter Communications, Inc.
1120 Avenue of the Americas
New York, New York 10036

1

Martha Batten's cottage, which had once been a cattle shippen, stood high on a hill overlooking the sheltered valley of Penscombe in East Devon. There was a stream nearby, and a plot of ground where Martha could grow vegetables and keep a few goats and hens. A copse gave protection from the south-westerly winds which, spray-laden, roared up over the precipitous cliff. It was a snug enough place and the old woman would have been well content but for her perpetual anxiety over her beloved Miss Jocelyn.

Jocelyn Harmer had been Martha's favourite of the three children at Penn Barton Manor where she had been employed as nurse. William, the only son, had taken pride of place with his parents. Rosamund, the eldest, fair-haired and blue-eyed, had been her grandfather's pet, and because Nathaniel Harmer's word was law at Penn Barton and Rosamund could twist him around her little finger, the whole household had been subject to her every whim.

Alone in her isolated cottage, Martha often found herself re-living the past. This warm spring morning she sat knitting in her doorway and sighed as memories crowded into her mind.

It had been spring, she recalled when the family had gone on that fateful visit to Exeter, taking with them Mrs. Harmer's new lady's maid and leaving Martha behind. As if a slip of a girl could keep an eye on Miss Rosamund, Martha had declared scornfully to cook as she watched the carriage disappear round a bend in the narrow lane which led to the highway.

'There'll be trouble, you mark my words,' she had predicted, and she had been right.

Rosamund, without even her youngest sister Jocelyn being aware of what she was doing, had contrived to meet secretly a young actor, one of a company of strolling players giving performances in the city. A week after the family's return to Penn Barton, she had run away, leaving a note in her untidy writing telling her parents that, certain of their disapproval of the man with whom she had fallen deeply in love, she had decided to elope with him.

It had happened ten years ago, yet to Martha it seemed like yesterday. Mrs. Harmer had wept and wrung her hands. Mr. Harmer had made exhaustive enquiries, offered a reward for information, relentlessly questioned twelve-year-old Jocelyn, but to no purpose. For she was as stunned as everyone else by Rosamund's disappearance and had known nothing of her sister's secret lover. Above all, Martha remembered old Nathaniel Harmer's reaction. For a while it seemed he might lose his reason. The doctor had bled him repeatedly. The parson had tried to calm him. But, since Rosamund herself was the only person who could ever bring a smile to his lips or gentleness into his voice, all attempts to placate him had failed. For seventeen years he had doted on the pretty, wayward child, and she had left him, without a word; without, apparently, a moment's regret.

He forbade her name ever to be mentioned. He ordered her portrait to be turned face to the wall. He became meaner, more irascible than ever. When Jocelyn had been left an orphan at fifteen, her brother William already dead, Nathaniel had made her swear solemnly on the family Bible that she would never leave him. Since then he had kept her tied hand and foot, permitting her no friends or social life, and not a penny above her meagre dress allowance.

Martha laid aside her knitting and rose. It was time to collect the eggs which she supplied to Penn Barton Manor. Jocelyn would be here soon to fetch them. Not for the first time Martha wished she could fill the basket with poisonous toadstools or berries of deadly nightshade for Jocelyn to take to her grandfather instead of his favourite brown eggs. And often, when alone, she would shake her fist and talk aloud to the absent Rosamund, telling her just what she thought of the way she had made her younger sister suffer for her own misdeeds. No one knew even if Rosamund was alive. She had written one letter only, to Jocelyn, a year after her disappearance. It gave no hint of her whereabouts, but told of her marriage, the birth of a son, and of her own happiness. There was no word of regret or repentance, and Jocelyn, obeying her grandfather's order that Rosamund's name should never be mentioned, had kept the letter to herself.

When she returned from the hen-house, Martha caught sight of Jocelyn a little way beyond the gate. The girl was absorbed in watching the flight of a pair the peregrine falcons which nested each year on the cliffs. She was wearing a green gown with yellow bows on the bodice and lace flounces at the elbows. The wide yellow ribbon of her straw hat was tied beneath her chin.

When the birds had flown out of sight, she turned and came on up the cliff path. Martha's face softened as it always did when she greeted this tall, dark-haired girl with the wide grey eyes.

'What a beautiful day!' Jocelyn exclaimed as she opened the little wicket gate. 'I was wishing I might stay out all morning.'

'So you should be able to,' Martha declared. 'Instead of having to go back to Penn Barton so that you're there for your grandfather to vent his spleen on as soon as he comes downstairs. 'Tis downright wicked, the way he keeps you so tied.'

'He has always been afraid I might follow Rosamund's example, and so leave him quite alone.'

The peregrines reappeared, the tercel chasing his mate above the copse. Jocelyn's eyes were wistful as she followed the swift flight of the birds.

'I suppose that, given the chance, I might have fallen head-over-heels in love just as Rosamund did. But now . . .' She turned to her old nurse and spread her hands in a helpless gesture. 'Now it would be the worst possible thing to happen, would it not?'

'Because of this contract of marriage your grandfather made with that dry stick of a lawyer from Honiton?'

Jocelyn admonished her gently. 'You must not speak of Mr. Creedy like that, Martha. He is kind enough in his way, and treats me with great respect.'

'Respect!' Martha's tone was scornful. ''Tis not respect you should be having at your age. What you need is a young man with some spirit in him, to take you by the hand and run you up the hillside and kiss you while you've no breath to say him nay. That's what you need, Miss Jocelyn. Instead . . .' She removed a snail from the base of a lavender bush and trod on it fiercely. 'Instead, as soon as you're no longer tied to your grandfather, you're to be married off to a man of forty-four who's had two wives already and never a child from either of them. Oh, they've planned it well to suit themselves! Your grandfather has you to look after him in his old age and doesn't pay a penny for all those law suits he delights in. And Mr. Creedy will get a young wife and a fine dowry to go with her.' Angrily she tugged at a dead branch of the lavender bush.

Jocelyn put a hand on the old woman's arm. 'Martha, hush! You must not talk in that way.'

'And why not, pray? I'm no longer in Mr. Harmer's

employ and can have my say. Although,' she added a little doubtfully, 'seeing that it's his cottage I live in and he'd not think twice about throwing me out tomorrow if I displeased him, I'd best guard my tongue. 'Tis just that I'm so grieved for you, ma'am.'

'I know.' Jocelyn put an arm around Martha's shoulders. 'You are a great comfort to me, Martha.' Her tone changed. 'But let us not think about the future on such a lovely day. The primroses and violets are in bloom and the birds building nests in every hedgerow. And Farmer Blakiston's black mare has just foaled.' She caught hold of Martha's hands. 'It is spring, and I always feel light-hearted in the spring. One day I shall no longer be living in Penscombe, to see the joy of new life as it spreads all over the valley, but until that day comes, let us make the best of things.'

The old woman stood on tiptoe to kiss Jocelyn's cheek. 'You're right, my dear. I shouldn't have spoken as I did. And, to be sure, 'tis a long time since I've seen you with so much colour in your cheeks and sparkle in your eyes, just as you had as a child.' She handed Jocelyn the basket of eggs. 'Here you are, ma'am, two dozen, all brown ones just as the master likes them. Will you stop for a drink of goat's milk?'

Jocelyn shook her head. 'I had better not. I dawdled on my way here, there was so much to look at.'

As she made her way down the cliff path, Jocelyn continued to look about her with appreciation. The sea, deep blue and green, lapped gently at the smooth pebbles of the beach far below her. A few fishermen were down there, mending their nets or preparing crab pots. On the opposite side of the combe the cliffs rose sharply, almost white where the red sandstone gave way to chalk. Sheep grazed amongst the furze and stunted bushes of sloe and hawthorn, calling reassuringly to their lambs whose bleating mingled with the sharp cries of jackdaws and the screaming of gulls. From the little wood above the water meadows a cuckoo called.

Jocelyn was singing softly to herself as she approached the stile. Then she stopped abruptly.

There was a young man sitting on the stile, a stranger. But he affected ignorance of her presence and, raising the telescope which lay across his knees, peered intently out to sea.

Jocelyn frowned. A stranger with a telescope boded no good for the village. There was scarcely a family which was not in some way involved in 'the trade'. For those who knew how to recognise the signs, such as bottle ends embedded in the walls of certain houses to show they offered a hiding-place in an emergency, or footprints in the wet earth of paths which led, apparently, nowhere in particular, it was easy enough to tell that smuggling played a large part in the life of Penscombe.

Suspiciously, Jocelyn studied the stranger, while his attention was still directed towards the sea. Although he was perched on the stile with his knees drawn up, she could see that he was tall. He wore a blue suit of good quality, with silver braiding along the edges of cuffs and pockets; white stockings and silver-buckled black shoes. His shirt looked to be of fine linen and there was a heavy gold ring, bearing a crest, on the third finger of the hand which gripped the telescope. He was bare-headed and his hair, of a rich auburn colour, was tied with a wide black ribbon. He was too well-dressed to be the new Preventive Officer, Jocelyn decided. But if he was a gentleman, he was not worthy of the description, since he was so deliberately keeping her waiting.

She cleared her throat loudly and stepped forward. The man turned, affecting surprise at sight of her. He swung his long legs over the stile and made her a low bow.

'Your pardon, ma'am. I was not aware that I was blocking the path of a charming young lady.'

Her annoyance at the untruth died away as he smiled at her. His face was tanned, suggesting he lived much in the open, and there were fine lines at the outer corners of his eyes as if he narrowed them against the sun's glare. Or they might have been caused by laughter, Jocelyn thought. In fact, his whole appearance gave the impression of a young man to whom life was a pleasant, carefree affair.

Jocelyn found herself returning his smile. 'You were obviously engrossed in your observations,' she said.

'I was watching that ship.' He pointed out to sea. 'A French brigantine, with very fine lines to her.' He proffered his telescope. 'Would you care to take a look?'

From force of habit, Jocelyn was about to decline. She had been brought up to regard conversation with a strange man as the greatest impropriety. Rosamund had broken that rule, but she herself had rarely been tempted to do so. Now, there seemed no harm in it at all.

She said, 'Thank you. I would, very much. But I do not know much about ships, except for the local fishing smacks.'

'Ships are my life,' he said, and she detected pride in his voice. 'Let me adjust the telescope for you, and then I will explain that vessel's rig.'

He took Jocelyn's basket and placed it carefully on the grass, then stood very close beside her, holding the telescope steady.

'She's a fine ship,' he said again, 'though I have no cause to admire a French vessel. I have suffered too many times at their hands.'

Jocelyn would have liked to learn more about him. But as she handed back the telescope, her foot touched her basket and she was reminded that she had already delayed her return to Penn Barton longer than she had intended.

'I must go now,' she said urgently. 'I am already late, and ...'

'You will be out of favour with your husband?'

'I have no husband,' she answered a little primly. 'It is my grandfather ...'

'Ah, I understand,' he said, glancing at her basket. 'You are on an errand of mercy? 'Tis a sad thing to grow old, to become feeble and ...'

'Oh, he is not really feeble. But he ...'

How could she explain to this amiable young man the irascible character of her grandfather?

He put her basket on the other side of the stile, then vaulted lightly over. Jocelyn gathered up her skirt and climbed on to the narrow step. She saw the stranger glance appreciatively at the yellow stockings revealed above her serviceable brown shoes. He took hold of her hand. His fingers were warm and strong. He was smiling broadly, his blue eyes very bright. She had not supposed that being helped over a stile could be so pleasant and amusing. She smiled back and attempted to jump lightly from the step. Her foot caught in her skirt. She lost her balance and fell against the young man. To her confusion, she found herself held close against him, her cheek against his chest, her straw hat tilted backwards.

He burst out laughing. 'That was excellently done. You chose exactly the right moment.'

Jocelyn exclaimed indignantly, 'You surely did not think I tripped on purpose?'

'Of course I did. And why not? 'Tis an old trick and I have nothing but admiration for your performance.'

She tried to pull away from him. 'Sir, I do assure you, I had not the slightest intention ...'

'Then I am vastly disappointed, for I had always supposed myself to be ...' He paused, and looked more closely at her. 'Why, what is the matter? You appear to be quite shocked.' Abruptly he released her and stepped back. 'I ask your pardon. I had not meant to offend you in the slightest.'

Jocelyn, helplessly shaking her head, said, 'It is just that . . .'

But she was unable to explain. For he was quite right. She *was* shocked, but not by his behaviour. It was her own feelings which had so startled her. In her confusion, Martha's words came to mind:

'What you need is a young man with spirit to take you by the hand and run you up the hillside and kiss you while you've no breath to say him nay.'

She was ashamed to realise that if this young man *had* attempted to kiss her, she would not have wanted to resist.

Her fingers were trembling as she righted her hat and re-tied the ribbons. The young man handed her the basket. His eyes were troubled and there was uncertainty in his voice.

'You are obviously distressed, and I must have been the cause. I am truly sorry. I have been long at sea, starved of the sight of a pretty woman. As you came down the hill, you looked delightfully young and gay, like the very spirit of spring in your green and yellow gown, that I . . .' In the wood, a cuckoo called. The stranger gave Jocelyn a rueful smile. 'It would seem that fellow has me summed up.'

Feeling foolish and embarrassed, Jocelyn attempted an explanation.

'There is no need for you to apologise. Truly, I have taken no offence. But my grandfather does not allow me to speak to strangers and . . .' She broke off, growing even more confused by the incredulity in his eyes. 'The fact is,' she went on desperately, only too aware how absurd the words must sound, 'that he will be very angry if I delay any longer.'

'Then at least allow me to escort you down this steep path.'

She shook her head. 'It is kind of you, but I dare not. We might be seen.'

Again she saw astonishment in his face.

'You sound like someone in a story-book,' he said in obvious perplexity. 'A princess, shut up by an ogre in a dark tower. May I not even know your name?'

'It can be of no consequence,' she said, and wondered if he heard the regret in her voice. 'Nor yours to me. I bid you good-day, sir.'

Although she withstood the temptation to look back as she hurried down the cliff path, Jocelyn was fully conscious that he was watching her until, when she opened the gate to Farmer Blakiston's water meadow, she was out of his sight. Hastening back to Penn Barton, she was painfully aware that, although she might never see this young man again, he had opened for her a door which, in her circumstances, it would have been better to have kept tightly closed.

Jocelyn stood at the open window of her bedroom, delaying as long as possible the moment when she must go down to the drawing-room. She had changed into a high-necked, dark silk gown with collar and cuffs of locally made lace. Her thick black hair was gathered into a filet on her neck.

I look as prim as a governess, she thought, regarding her reflection with distaste. Neither the clothes nor hair style were of her choosing, but what her grandfather considered suitable when she received Thomas Creedy. Since her prospective husband was middle-aged it was necessary, it seemed, that she should camouflage her own youth as much as possible.

She sighed as she looked out of the window. The slopes of the combe were so steep that for several hours each day one side was always in shadow. In the morning the sun shone full into her bedroom. Now, it was sinking behind the trees on the hills above Penn Barton, and its shafts fell upon the opposite slope, turning the sheep pink and enhancing the brightness of the gorge. Slowly, as she watched, the shadows lengthened, dusk moved up the hillside. The last building to be illumined by the sun's rays was Galliards, the Elizabethan mansion standing on a small plateau in the shelter of Hawkwood. The wood, so it was said, was haunted by the ghost of a Cavalier who had vainly sought refuge there from the pursuit of the Roundheads. The Cavalier had been Sir John Peverell; the leader of the Cromwellians, Edmund Harmer. It had happened over a century earlier. Yet in the mind of Nathaniel Harmer, Edmund's grandson, those times of hatred and violence still lived on. While there were still Peverells living at Galliards, he had spent hours glaring across the valley, devising ways of doing them harm. But the house had been empty these twenty years, since the Penscombe branch of the family had died out.

To Jocelyn the deserted house and grounds had been a place of enchantment. Many times in childhood she had crept up the overgrown drive and peered through the windows festooned with cobwebs. Creepers grew unchecked over the walls. Bats and mice inhabited the dilapidated barns. Rabbits and foxes made their homes in holes hidden by the tangled vegetation.

Sometimes Jocelyn's brother William had accompanied her on these expeditions. But his inclination had been more towards reading. After he went away to boarding-school she had seen little of him, for even in the holidays he seemed always to have his head buried in a book. All his studying had come to naught. A week after his thirteenth birthday he had ridden out reluctantly beside his father to join the hunt, and returned, carried on a field gate, his body hidden beneath his father's coat.

Jocelyn watched from her window until the last rays of the sun caught the very crest of the hill. Then the bird-song, which filled the valley each spring evening, lessened. She closed the window, picked up her reticule and made her way downstairs. On the lower landing she paused. Although she had seen it every day for ten years, the sight of her sister's portrait, turned to face the wall, still had power to sadden her. Sometimes, when she was sure her grandfather was not about, she would lift it away from the wall and take a quick peep.

She wondered how different Rosamund looked now from this pretty girl with the fair ringlets, big blue eyes and pouting mouth. Perhaps Rosamund's husband had become a well-known actor, or had left the stage for some more lucrative career. Perhaps they were no longer in England. Did Rosamund, Jocelyn wondered, ever give a thought to her younger sister whose life, by her impulsive act, she had unwittingly caused to become so restricted and cheerless?

The door of the drawing-room was open and Jocelyn could see her grandfather and Thomas Creedy sitting before the fire, their heads bent over the chess-board. At eighty-one, Nathaniel Harmer was a bent, wizened man, dressed always in black. On his bald head he wore a skull-cap. His heavy wig was kept on a stand beside him, ready to be put on when any special visitor called.

Thomas, who no longer rated as a special visitor, was wearing a new suit of brown velvet with a gold waist-coat. His wig had been carefully combed and powdered, and he had changed from riding-boots into highly polished black shoes. His stockings and cravat were immaculately white, his nails manicured. There were women, Jocelyn supposed, who would be proud to be betrothed to this man of high principles, orderly habits and punctilious manners. She was not one of them.

She had never seen him laugh. All he ever managed

was a frosty smile. Her attempts to prove to him that she was capable of holding an intelligent conversation had been unsuccessful. In Thomas Creedy's view, it seemed, a woman's place was, not at a man's side, but at least one pace behind him, and the more silently she followed him through life, the better.

Yet, if she was to become his wife—and in that she had no choice—she must persevere in looking for his good qualities. She must curb her irritation at his precise speech and dry little cough, and give up hoping to discover some warmth in his nature.

She waited in the doorway until her grandfather had completed his move, then joined the two players. Thomas rose to greet her. As he held out his hand, she experienced the familiar sense of revulsion she had tried so hard to overcome. When they were married, she knew it would take all her will power not to shrink from him. How differently she had reacted to the clasp of the young stranger's hand as he helped her over the stile.

Shocked at the recollection, she forced a smile as she curtsied to Thomas.

Her grandfather remarked testily, 'You have interrupted our game, Jocelyn.'

She answered patiently, 'I am sorry, sir. I understood you had requested me to join you.'

'Yes, yes, of course. But you should have come earlier or waited until we had finished.' He glanced at Thomas. 'Go on, sir, make your move. Jocelyn can amuse herself by giving us some music while we finish our game, provided she does not play loudly enough to put me off.'

Thomas pulled out the stool which stood against the spinet. 'It will give me great pleasure to hear you play,' he said with formal politeness.

'Come along, come along,' Nathaniel muttered irritably. 'I want my supper. But I'm determined to beat you before I have it.'

Jocelyn played quietly, pieces she knew well so that her thoughts were free to wander. They led her down to the cliff path where, for a few brief moments, she had recaptured the carefree spirit of her youth. What harm was there in re-living those moments? She did not suppose she would ever see the young man again. But at least she could keep him in her memory, like summer sunshine recalled on a grey winter day.

When the game of chess ended, she went with the two men into the dining-room. It was a dark room, oak-panelled. Her grandfather insisted on the curtains being drawn the moment the light began to fade; yet his meanness would not allow sufficient candles to be lit. But, even at his advanced age, he enjoyed his meals, so that the table was well laden, the wines excellent. Thomas tucked his napkin into the neck of his cravat, waited for Nathaniel to pronounce grace, then set to with relish.

Neither he nor the old man talked when they were eating, their whole concentration being on their food. Jocelyn was forced to maintain the same silence, allowed only to speak to the maidservant who waited upon them. She supposed she would have to suffer these dreary meal-times for the rest of her life—unless she had children. Although it seemed natural and desirable to raise a family, the thought of bearing Thomas's children gave her no pleasure. In any case, she had no notion whatever of how to deal with babies. Occasionally she would stop to talk to a child in the village, or smile at a toddler clinging to its mother's skirts. But they were shy of her, and she of them.

Thomas folded his napkin and laid it carefully on the table.

'An excellent meal, sir, excellent. I am much obliged to you, and to Miss Jocelyn, who doubtless had the ordering of it.'

She inclined her head in acknowledgment and, casting

an enquiring glance at her grandfather and receiving his
assent, rose and returned to the drawing-room. She saw
by the clock on the mantelpiece that there remained several tedious hours yet to be endured before Thomas set
out on his ride back to Honiton. Not until he left could
she gain the privacy of her bed-room and lose herself in
one of Mr. Henry Fielding's novels.

When the two men joined her, she could see at once
that something had upset her grandfather. She was not
long in learning what it was.

'Mr. Creedy's just given me a most provoking piece of
news,' he told her as she handed him his favourite pipe.
'He says those damned Peverells are coming back to Galliards.'

Jocelyn turned to Thomas in surprise. 'Is that true?'

He sat forward, hands on knees. 'Perfectly true.'

'But I thought the family had died out.'

'So they have,' Nathaniel said impatiently. 'The Penscombe branch, that is, and 'twas good riddance to 'em as
far as I was concerned. But it seems there's a great-
nephew or distant cousin—it don't signify—who's decided
to renovate the house and install himself there.'

Jocelyn glanced at Thomas. 'May I ask when you heard
this?'

'A few days since. The young man was in Honiton,
making enquiries about stone-masons and discussing the
legal side with Samuel Cartwright.' His mouth turned
down at the corners. 'Cartwright, of all people! I should
have thought a man in Captain Peverell's position would
have come at once to me.'

'*Captain* Peverell?' Jocelyn repeated.

'So he styles himself. It appears he was left a merchant
fleet by his father. He does very well out of it, by the impression he gave Cartwright—so well that he's turning
his back on the sea for a while in order to play at being a
country gentleman.'

19

Jocelyn sat very still, her head bent. 'I have been so long at sea,' the young man had said. 'Ships are my whole life.'

Her grandfather's angry outburst broke into her thoughts. 'He'll be a King's man, a damned Cavalier. All the Peverells are.'

'The Civil War ended over a hundred years ago,' Jocelyn reminded him. 'Nobody gives any thought to it nowadays.'

The old man jerked up his head. 'I do. Always shall. And we can do without those simpering dandies in Penscombe. They're all of a piece, the Peverells, irresponsible, arrogant popinjays.'

Thomas cleared his throat. 'I scarcely think, sir, that a young man who controls a fleet of ships can be described . . .'

'I didn't ask for your opinion. You've been in this district less than twenty years. You're as much of a "foreigner" as the new Preventive Officer.'

Thomas remained silent, but his thin lips tightened. Jocelyn rose and went to the spinet, not wanting either of them to observe how interested she was in what Thomas had said. After a few moments he spoke again, peevishly. 'I suppose, although he has never set foot in the district until now, that Captain Peverell will not be regarded as a "foreigner". And a wealthy bachelor is always welcome in certain quarters, even though I dare say his manners will be as coarse as those of your yeoman farmers, after his years at sea.'

'Oh, no,' Jocelyn protested incautiously.

'What was that?' her grandfather demanded, cupping a hand to his ear.

'I . . .' She gave a little nervous laugh. 'I was talking to myself, deciding that this piece of music would not be suitable.'

To her relief, her explanation was accepted, although

Thomas eyed her doubtfully. Hastily she sat down and began to play. Her fingers seemed out of control and she heard herself striking wrong notes. Thomas rose and came to her side.

'Miss Jocelyn, you appear to be a trifle indisposed. You have, perhaps, been affected by the sudden heat, so early in the year.'

'I think that may be so,' she said, grateful for the excuse. 'I am a little fatigued.'

'How can you be fatigued, at your age?' Nathaniel demanded. 'Young people nowadays have no stamina. As for me, I'm as fit at eighty as I ever was. I'll take you on again, Creedy.'

The lawyer bowed stiffly. 'Thank you, sir, but I think it is time I took my leave. It is a long ride home, as you know.'

The old man snorted. 'Huh! Used to ride twice as far as that when I was a young man. But then, you're not so young, are you?'

His guest drew himself up. 'I do not consider just over forty as being particularly old,' he said haughtily. 'And I congratulate myself that I have kept in excellent health by orderly and abstemious living.'

His host studied him from beneath shaggy eyebrows. 'You've the figure of a younger man, I'll grant you that. Whether you've enough spark in you to father a family, remains to be seen.'

Thomas pinched in his nostrils. 'That, sir,' he said coldly, 'is scarcely a proper subject to be mentioned in front of Miss Jocelyn.'

Nathaniel drew on his pipe and puffed out a cloud of smoke. 'Don't be such a prude, Creedy. Jocelyn has lived in the country all her life. She's well aware of the methods God ordained for procreating life. Whether she'll ever experience them, I have my doubts. But I'll be dead by that time, so I'll never know. Go home, then, if you want to. For myself, I never go to bed before midnight, though I dare say it puts a few more pence on the house-keeping for candles.'

Thomas's face was set as Jocelyn went with him into the hall. She called for a maidservant to bring his boots and help him on with his riding-coat.

She asked lightly, 'We are to expect you as usual on Sunday, after church?'

His tone was coldly formal. It was obvious he was still greatly offended by the old man's words. 'Certainly, ma'am. I greatly look forward to Sundays at Penn Barton.'

Which is more than I do, Jocelyn thought. For her, Sunday was a day to be endured. First, the long sermon delivered by the ageing, absent-minded parson. Then the slow walk back to the house with her grandfather leaning on her arm, followed by a silent meal, and the two men snoring in the library all afternoon.

When the door had shut behind Thomas, Jocelyn returned to the drawing-room. Nathaniel was staring at the chess-board. Suddenly he swept all the pieces on to the floor.

'That's what I'd have done with the whole pack of them, the damned Cavaliers!'

Jocelyn saw by his eyes that he was absorbed in one of his favourite pastimes, re-living the bitter days of the Civil War, in which, had he been born a century earlier, he would have been so much at home.

She asked quietly, 'Have I your permission to retire now?'

He nodded absent-mindedly. 'So there's to be a Peverell again at Galliards,' he muttered. 'A wealthy Peverell, and unmarried. *Jocelyn.*'

Startled, she turned at the door. 'Sir?'

He wagged an admonitory finger at her. 'If you ever chance to encounter this fellow, you're not to speak to

22

him. Not a single word. D'you understand?'

For one wild, rebellious moment she was tempted to declare, 'You are too late, Grandfather. I have already spoken to him. I hope that I shall have the chance to do so again, many times.'

Instead, she inclined her head and said dutifully, 'I understand.'

Collecting a candle from the hall table, she went slowly up the stairs, past the inverted portrait of her sister who had, for better or worse, made her escape, and along the dark passage to her bedroom. When she had undressed and climbed into the four-poster bed that was much too big to sleep in alone, she blew out her candle. For she knew that Mr. Fielding's *Tom Jones* would have no power to hold her interest this night.

Next morning, the weather was again as warm as summer. Jocelyn put on a faded dress of sprigged muslin, braided her hair to keep it tidy, and went out to weed the herb garden. After a while, she became aware of unfamiliar sounds from across the valley: hammering and banging, and the rhythmic scrape of a saw.

Looking through a gap in the old stone wall, she saw immediately the cause of the noise. A wagon was drawn up before the front door of Galliards, and workmen were busy about the place.

Jocelyn returned to her weeding, but her mind was no longer on her task. She was picturing those cob-webby rooms freshly decorated. There would be carpets and furniture and exotic drapes and tapestries, perhaps, brought from foreign lands in Captain Peverell's own ships.

Jocelyn glanced up at the window of her grandfather's bedroom. The shutters were still tightly closed. He rarely rose before midday. Brushing the earth from her hands, Jocelyn walked quickly through the orchard, then entered the little copse at the end of the garden. She crossed the stream by a fallen branch and scrambled up the bank. Not for years had she followed this secret way, but she easily found the path which led to the track the smugglers used, then branched off and climbed up the hillside. From the clump of trees just above Galliards she had a splendid view of house and grounds. Sitting on a cushion of moss, she drew up her knees and clasped her hands around them.

Below her, about a score of men were at work, repairing the stonework and timbers, clearing overgrown creepers from windows, scything the long grass and cutting back straggling briars. Some of them she recognised, men from the village. But the stone-masons were strangers; from Honiton, she guessed. A boy, carrying an armful of kindling, came out of a shed and lit a bonfire.

Jocelyn was totally absorbed in these activities. She wondered if the young man with the humorous blue eyes was down there, directing the workmen; and hugged her knees more tightly, chuckling to herself as she thought how astonished he would be if he could see her now.

Suddenly, behind her, there was an ear-splitting report. She sprang to her feet, the acrid smell of gun-powder in her nostrils. A wood pigeon fluttered down from a tree a few yards away.

A man stepped from behind a bush and walked over to retrieve the bird. For a moment, through the smoke, Jocelyn did not recognise him. Then, with dismay, she saw that it was Captain Peverell. She stood very still, holding her breath, fearing discovery. For how, without acute embarrassment, could she explain her presence here?

The bird still jerked convulsively. Captain Peverell bent and killed it, swiftly and humanely. Then, in a leisurely fashion, he cleaned and re-loaded his gun.

He wore a hat this morning, a brown tricorne set at a

jaunty angle on his auburn hair. He had his back to Jocelyn, but she noticed how he stood with legs braced as if he were still on board ship. She could hear him whistling as he completed his task. Then he picked up the pigeon and moved away. Jocelyn sighed inwardly with relief. Then something—it could have been a spider or merely a leaf—tickled her neck. Involuntarily she uttered a little cry and slapped at the object.

The young man swung round. Jocelyn pressed herself against a tree trunk, but there was no longer any hope of remaining unseen. He walked slowly towards her, astonishment changing into recognition.

'Are you not the same young lady I met on the cliff path yesterday?' he asked.

She nodded unhappily. She was becoming painfully conscious of her faded gown with its muddied skirt; that her braid had come loose and a thick strand of hair was falling untidily on to her shoulder. She realised, too, that her hands were stained with earth. Her cheeks grew hot and she wished fervently that she had not yielded to such a foolish impulse.

Captain Peverell was regarding her with a half-puzzled, half amused air.

'I suppose, ma'am, since you are not allowed to speak to strangers, the kindest action on my part would be to walk away and leave you. But this does happen to be my property.'

'Yes, I know,' she said hastily. 'I assure you, I meant no harm.'

He put his head on one side. 'I had not suspected you of poaching.'

She drew a deep breath. 'If you must know, I was . . .' Under his amused scrutiny she hesitated; then, with a show of bravado, she burst out, 'I was watching the work being done at your house. Doubtless it was very foolish and . . .'

'Certainly it was,' he agreed equably. 'For if you had come and asked me, I would have shown you exactly what is being done.'

'Oh, I could not have done that!'

'Of course, I had forgotten,' he said with mock solemnity. 'It would have displeased the ogre, your grandfather. I must confess, however, that you puzzle me. You are forbidden to hold a perfectly harmless conversation with a man because you have not been formally introduced. Yet you roam about the countryside, unchaperoned, dressed like a . . .'

'A dairy-maid?' she finished for him. 'I have been gardening.'

'A most worthy occupation. Might I ask where your garden lies?'

She made a vague gesture, 'Over there, on the far side of the valley.'

'And you live with your grandfather?'

'Yes. And I must return at once. If he discovers my absence he will . . .'

'Lock you in your room with nothing but bread and water? Or banish you from beneath his roof, never to return?'

She bent her head. 'I think you are laughing at me.'

'You do not like being laughed at?'

She answered gravely, 'I have had no experience of it, since my childhood.'

He stepped forward and looked closely at her. 'How long is it since you laughed at yourself—or at anything, for that matter?' When she did not answer he said gently, 'I am sorry, I appear to have offended you again. Perhaps I have been over-long at sea and forgotten how to behave towards young ladies. Let us start afresh, by a formal introduction.' He swept off his hat and made her a low bow. 'Adam Peverell, merchant captain, aged twenty-six, a bachelor of untarnished reputation as vouched for by my sisters, at your service.'

Despite herself, Jocelyn could not help laughing. He looked relieved.

'Now it is your turn,' he said. 'To tell me your name, I mean.'

'I am Jocelyn Harmer, of Penn Barton Manor. And if my grandfather should ever hear that I had spoken to you, he would be exceedingly angry.'

'But why? What is so dreadful about it?'

She decided to tell him the truth. 'Apart from the fact that you are a stranger ...'

'No longer,' he reminded her. 'We have just introduced ourselves.'

'Apart from that,' she continued doggedly. 'You are a Peverell, a Cavalier.'

'I beg your pardon?' He looked taken aback.

'I know it sounds foolish. But your family were for King Charles, mine for Cromwell. There has been a rift ever since.'

'You cannot be serious,' he declared, his eyes widening with astonishment.

'But I am, perfectly serious.'

'You mean that the Civil War is still fought here, well over a hundred years after it ended? No, I cannot believe it.'

'You have not met my grandfather,' she said ruefully.

'If what you say of him is true, I have not the slightest desire to do so. Why, however old he may be, he could not even have been born at the time.'

'That is of no consequence to him. You know, perhaps, that one of your ancestors, Sir John Peverell, was killed in the wood behind your house, and is supposed to haunt it still?'

He nodded curtly. 'I have heard the tale.'

'He was struck down by a Harmer. In the next generation the Peverells took their revenge. After that, there was no more killing, but the hatred continued. I think, in a way, my grandfather was disappointed when the Penscombe branch of your family died out and he could no longer glare across the valley and utter curses upon anyone of your name. So you will see why . . .'

'I never heard anything so absurd! Surely *you* do not subscribe to this ridiculous feud?'

'Should I be talking to you now, if I did? And, indeed, I must not do so any longer.'

Firmly refusing his offer to escort her home, Jocelyn made her way, as quickly as she could, along the smugglers' path and across the stream. She was out of breath when she reached the garden, and sank thankfully on to a seat. She had scarcely been there a minute or two before Polly, the freckle-faced maid whom Jocelyn had rescued from the poorhouse, came running towards her, bursting with importance.

'Oh, ma'am, I wondered wherever you'd gone!' she exclaimed when she reached her mistress.

'What has happened?' Jocelyn asked anxiously. 'My grandfather . . . ?'

'He'm still abed, the Lord be praised. 'Tis this, ma'am.' Dramatically she drew a letter from beneath her apron.

'For me?' Jocelyn held out her hand.

'Yes,' Polly said in awe. 'And 'tis so rare a thing for you to get a letter, Cook and me thought it might be something special.'

Jocelyn glanced with curiosity at the inscription. Then she stiffened. Even after nine years, it was easy to recognise her sister's untidy handwriting. She dismissed Polly, who went away, disappointed. Her fingers were trembling as she spread out the letter.

My dearest sister, she read, *Nothing but the direst necessity would make me throw myself upon your mercy. Even so, it is not for my own sake, but my son's. The* writing was not only spidery, but blotched with ink, and Jocelyn had great difficulty in deciphering the words. *At the end of last year my dear husband was taken from me by the smallpox, which I also caught, but recovered. Now I have a lung infection and am told there is no hope. Even as I write this I am in a high fever and it is difficult . . .*

There was a large blot, making the next few words impossible to read. Then the writing became a little clearer.

I pray you to have pity on my child, though you may have none for me. I neither want nor deserve any . . . I have been so very happy. Sometimes Malcolm did well and we lived comfortably, at others we were very poor. Always his thought was for me and the children. I had two little girls as well as Paul, but they are dead, I cannot remember of what illness. I am so confused. Sometimes they seem to be here with me, and Papa and Mama, and you and William. Yet I have had news that only you are left. That is why I ask your protection for my son . . . a wagon bound for Seaton will stop at the Hangmanstone cross-roads on Saturday evening. I beg you, meet it there. I can send no money—nothing . . .

The sentence trailed off. Just above Rosamund's scrawled signature a few more words were clear enough to be read. . . . *in your hands, I have not long to live.*

Jocelyn felt cold all over. She re-read the letter, rising to her feet in her agitation. Somehow she must get help to Rosamund. She looked for an address. There was none.

She hurried along the path, calling for Polly. The maid appeared so quickly that it was obvious she had been waiting around the corner of the house. Jocelyn questioned her anxiously.

'Who brought this letter?'

'A boy from the village, ma'am. He said a man riding along the highway gave him sixpence to deliver it, to save him riding down here himself.'

'Did he say who the man was—where he came from?'

The maid shook her head. 'The boy'd never seen him afore. 'Twas a stranger.'

'How long ago was this?'

Polly puckered her forehead. 'Almost an hour, I'd say.'

'And the boy? Do you know who he was, where he can be found?'

He was on his way down to join his father. They'll be away to the crab-pots by now.'

At a loss, Jocelyn dismissed the maid and began pacing up and down the path. It seemed that she was powerless to help her sister. As for Rosamund's son . . . Again she scanned the letter and saw, to her dismay, that the boy would be arriving the next day. But it would be useless for him to come. Nathaniel Harmer would never allow Rosamund's son at Penn Barton.

Yet how could he be stopped? Without an address, with no means of finding out Rosamund's whereabouts, she was helpless.

A sound from above brought her sharply back to the present. The shutters of her grandfather's bedroom were being pushed back; he would soon come downstairs. Friday was the day on which Jocelyn had to present her household accounts and the weekly list of purchases to be given to the carrier.

She hurried into the house to change her gown. While she hastily combed and pinned up her hair, she sought for some way out of the dilemma in which Rosamund's letter had placed her. But the picture of her pretty, wayward sister, near to death, apparently without money or friends and with a little boy entirely dependent upon her, clouded Jocelyn's mind so that she could not think clearly.

But she must do something, and quickly. Surely, in the circumstances, even such a vindictive old man as Nathaniel Harmer would show some forgiveness, some humanity? Screwing up her courage, Jocelyn went downstairs, rehearsing the words with which she would break the news and ask his help.

He was standing at the window of the little room which was used as office and writing-room, shaking his clenched fist at something she could not see. She heard him muttering.

'Stop that hammering! Have done with all that noise, you damned Cavaliers! I'll burn your house about your ears, that's what I'll do.'

As he turned and Jocelyn saw his face, his mouth thin-lipped, his straggling eyebrows drawn down in a heavy frown, her heart sank. Now was not the time to make her approach to him.

With the greatest difficulty she kept her patience throughout the weekly catechism on her management of the house; enduring his complaints, his suspicious questioning about a penny unaccounted for, his insistence that she must make it up out of her dress allowance.

Afterwards, she was grateful for the mealtime silence which gave her more chance to think. But by the end of luncheon she was no nearer a solution. And now her thoughts took a different turn. If, against all expectations, she did manage to persuade Nathaniel to take the boy in, what sort of life would it be for a child, in this house? Yet there was no other house to which he could go. He *must* come to Penn Barton.

The only solution was to keep his presence hidden until such time as she thought it possible to approach her grandfather. Jocelyn went upstairs and wandered from room to room, trying to think how it could be achieved. She came to the bedroom she had shared with Rosamund when they were little girls. She could picture her sister, curling her fair ringlets around her finger, preening herself before the mirror, while Martha . . .

Jocelyn almost cried out in relief. There was her answer. Martha would take the boy. She was always saying how much she missed having the care of children and that, old though she was, she reckoned she could manage them a sight better than some of these flighty young nursemaids she'd seen on a visit to Honiton.

Jocelyn put on her walking shoes and a hat. Now, while her grandfather was having his afternoon nap, she would go down and see Martha. Then she could meet this orphaned nephew with a plan already made.

2

Jocelyn was sitting on a pile of stones left by the way-warden for repairing the highway. She had been waiting for over an hour. The sun had gone down and it was quite cold here on the high ground above the sheltered combe. She pulled her cloak more closely about her and walked a little way along the road to the west. She did not like to go too far, in case the wagon bringing her nephew came, instead, from the north.

She had spent a busy and difficult day. It had taken a great deal of effort to persuade her grandfather to invite the parson to spend the evening with him, playing chess. Then she had discovered that the parson was away for the night. The only alternative was the doctor. If she could have thought of any other way of keeping her grandfather occupied for some hours so that he would not notice her absence, she would have taken it in preference to seeking help from Doctor Marsh. She had every respect for his skill as a physician, but she despised his weakness for wine. She disliked, too, his frequent innuendoes as to the real purpose of her walks, and his only partly-veiled suggestion that she was secretly meeting a lover when she visited Martha's cottage.

She had gone down to the cottage that morning long before her grandfather was stirring, to ask the old nurse if she would take Rosamund's son. Martha's reaction had been heart-warming. Her eyes, full of sympathy as she learned of Rosamund's plight, had lit up at the thought of having a child to care for again. It had been Jocelyn's plan, at first, to take her pony up to the Hangmanstone cross-roads, and ride with the boy to Martha's cottage. Then she realised that such an unusual sight would arouse curiosity. She had therefore decided to take the boy down the length of the valley by the hidden paths the smugglers used.

Now at last, in the distance, she saw a cloud of dust. She waited by the roadside, hands clasped tightly beneath her cloak, hoping that this might be the wagon on its way to Seaton.

A heavy vehicle with enormous wooden wheels, and covered with a canvas hood, came into view. It was drawn by six powerful horses, the waggoner riding alongside. Its progress was so slow that Jocelyn was tempted to run forward to meet it. But she waited until it drew up beside her. She stepped forward, coughing as the dust caught her throat.

'I am Miss Jocelyn Harmer,' she told the waggoner. 'I believe you have a boy . . .'

He nodded stolidly and rapped with his whip on the canvas hood.

'Wake up!' he shouted. 'You'm here.'

Dismounting, he went to the far side of the road to make some adjustment to the harness of one of his team. A boy jumped down from the back of the wagon and came slowly towards Jocelyn. He was tall for his age and very dark, with black hair and grey eyes, not in the least like Rosamund. He wore ankle-length blue trousers and a short jacket and he was carrying a small portmanteau.

As he came up to her, she said, 'You are Paul? I am your Aunt Jocelyn.' It sounded strange to her, said for the first time.

He regarded her gravely, then, remembering his manners, bowed. 'I am glad you have come, ma'am. I did not know whether Mama's letter would reach you in time.'

'It arrived yesterday.' Jocelyn held out her hand. 'Shall

I carry your portmanteau? We have quite a long way to walk.'

The boy kept tight hold of the handle. 'No, thank you, ma'am, I can manage. But—did you say, a long walk?'

'I am afraid so. Are you very tired?'

He shook his head, but there was a worried expression in his eyes. She began to explain where she was taking him, but was interrupted by the waggoner.

'Come on, boy,' he called roughly. 'Make haste and get 'em out.'

Jocelyn looked enquiringly at her nephew. 'What does he mean?'

The boy stared at the ground, rubbing his hand nervously on his trousers. When he did not answer, she questioned him again. He looked up at her, then quickly away. But she had seen a kind of desperation in his eyes. The words came out in a rush.

'Please, ma'am, I brought my sisters with me.'

Jocelyn gasped. 'Your—*sisters?*'

Paul nodded. 'Isabella and Sarah. They are asleep in the wagon.'

Jocelyn put her hands to her cheeks. 'But, I thought . . . Your mother wrote that . . .'

'There was only me left? I was afraid she might. She's very ill, you see, and she got muddled. She thought my sisters had died, like Papa. The man . . .' Paul jerked his head towards the waggoner. 'He thought there was only me, but I made him bring them as well. I told him . . . Please don't be angry, ma'am, but I had to say you would pay for them.'

Jocelyn shut her eyes, trying to take in this new and shattering development. She could hear the man cursing as he tightened a strap.

She felt a tug at her cloak. Opening her eyes, she found Paul was gazing at her beseechingly. His voice was high-pitched with anxiety.

'Please, ma'am, take them, too. Sarah's not a year old yet, she doesn't eat very much and Isabella . . .' He paused, frowning, then went on hastily, 'The man said he'd have to deliver them to the poorhouse if someone wasn't here to meet us, because they aren't old enough to work, like me.'

'I assure you, he will do no such thing,' she declared, horrified. 'Of course I will take them, Paul.'

The driver left his task and joined them as they went to the back of the wagon. Seeing his expectant expression, Jocelyn drew out her purse. Colouring, she emptied the contents into her hand.

'I am sorry,' she said, passing him the money. 'That is all I have.'

The man stared at the coins in disgust before thrusting them into the pocket of his smock.

'*You* can lift un down,' he said to Paul. 'And hurry up. I've lost enough time already with a broken trace.'

The boy clambered nimbly up on a wheel, and over the tailboard. Jocelyn reached up to take the baby Paul handed to her. Thankfully, she saw that the child was still asleep.

'That's Sarah,' Paul told her. Then he called over his shoulder, "Come on, Isabella, wake up.'

A girl of about four years old appeared at the tailboard. She was rubbing her eyes and sniffing.

'I want . . .' she began, but was cut short by her brother.

'Come *on*, Isabella. Aunt Jocelyn is waiting.'

The child opened her eyes wide and regarded Jocelyn with interest. They were large eyes, very blue, just like Rosamund's. Her ringlets, too, were like her mother's, soft and fair.

Jocelyn held out her hand. 'Come along, dear, the waggoner is anxious to be off.'

'I'm hungry,' Isabella announced.

'You're always saying you're hungry,' Paul said scathingly, 'but when you're given bread and milk you won't eat it.'

'I don't like bread and milk.'

'You won't even get that if you don't hurry,' Paul warned her, as the waggoner mounted his horse. 'I'm going to lift you down to Aunt Jocelyn. Stop making such a fuss.' Then, as Isabella still seemed about to protest, he added fiercely, 'I shall jump down and leave you.'

Immediately, Isabella put up her arms to be lifted down. With some difficulty Jocelyn managed to take the older girl from Paul. Isabella slithered to the ground and clutched at Jocelyn's cloak. Paul leaped lightly down. The waggoner shouted to his team and cracked his long whip over their backs. Jocelyn and the children were smothered in dust as the wagon went ponderously on its way.

Jocelyn asked, 'How far have you come, Paul?'

'From Plymouth. It seemed a very long way.'

'When did you last have anything to eat?'

'There was a farmer's wife in the wagon for a little while. She sat Sarah on her lap and gave us some bread. There was nothing left to eat in our room, after Mama . . .' He broke off, swallowing hard.

'Is your mother . . . ?'

Jocelyn did not complete her question, realising that even if there were any chance of helping Rosamund, it must wait. Her immediate task was to ensure these children were cared for. That, in itself, seemed wellnigh impossible. Even if she managed to get them to Martha's, how could that tiny cottage accommodate three children, and what would Martha's reaction be when faced with two little girls as well as the boy she expected?

Jocelyn became ware that Paul was gazing up into her face, waiting for her to make some positive move.

'Is it a very long way?' he asked. 'Because Isabella . . .'

'I will carry Isabella if she gets tired,' Jocelyn said, with a conviction she was far from feeling.

'I think you will not be able to carry both of them. I could manage Sarah for a little while.'

She smiled at him reassuringly. It was best that he did not realise how difficult was the journey before them; down stony paths, across two streams, up the steep cliff to Martha's cottage.

She settled the baby in the crook of her arm and took hold of Isabella's hand. The little girl held back and began to cry. Jocelyn, failing to quieten her, tried to drag her forward, wanting to be off the highway before anyone came upon them. Her efforts were of no avail.

Paul, reddening, said hesitantly, 'If you please, ma'am, I think she wants to go behind the hedge. And so do I.'

Jocelyn found a gateway and waited at the roadside until both children reappeared. Then she tried to persuade Isabella towards the overgrown lane leading off the highway.

The little girl stood her ground, complaining that she was hungry. The baby woke and began to whimper. Fervently Jocelyn wished Martha was with her. She tried rocking the baby, as she had seen the village women do.

'If you are a good girl,' she said to Isabella, 'you shall soon have something to eat.'

'I don't want . . .'

'Oh, do stop being so tiresome!' Paul exclaimed. 'If you don't behave, Aunt Jocelyn will leave you behind.'

This time his threat had a disastrous effect. Isabella knuckled her eyes. 'I want Mama,' she sobbed. 'You're horrid. I want Mama.'

Above the sound of her crying, Jocelyn heard the clip-clop of hooves.

'Quickly, down that lane,' she ordered Paul, and dragged Isabella forward.

The little girl's sobs turned to yells of frustration.

'There's a horse! I want to see the horse!'

Jocelyn lost her patience. Clasping Isabella around the waist, she tried to tuck the child under her arm. The little girl kicked, and screamed more loudly. Paul, turning to try and help, tripped over his portmanteau and fell sprawling in the dust. Isabella's fist caught her sister across the cheek. The baby's cries added to the commotion.

As the horseman reached them Jocelyn recognised Adam Peverell. There was an expression of utter astonishment on his face.

'I want to see the horse,' Isabella protested. 'Let me go! Let me go!'

Dismounting, Adam looped the reins over his arm. He managed to make himself heard above the clamour.

'You appear to be having some trouble, Miss Harmer. May I assist you?'

Feeling thoroughly humiliated, Jocelyn confessed, 'I am not used to children.'

'Then you must allow me to help,' he said, smiling, 'for I am very used to them, having a score of nephews and nieces.'

He took Isabella from Jocelyn and lifted her to his saddle. 'Now, be quiet,' he ordered her sternly.

The little girl gaped at him. Then, realising that she was actually mounted on a horse, her rebelliousness immediately changed to delight. She patted the animal's neck and beamed at Adam.

'Nice horse. Does it go fast?'

'When I want it to,' Adam replied equably. 'It won't go anywhere with you on its back if you don't behave yourself.'

Paul had picked himself up and was dusting down his trousers. The baby was still crying lustily despite Jocelyn's attempts to quieten her. Adam took out his watch and held it to Sarah's ear.

'Listen. Tick-tock. Tick-tock.'

The baby's cries lessened. She gazed solemnly at Adam while she listened to the watch. Then she chuckled and held out her arms. Adam laughed and took her from Jocelyn.

The sound of wheels came from along the highway. Jocelyn said hastily, 'Captain Peverell, I must not be seen.'

'With me?'

'Neither with you, nor these children.'

'Am I to suppose you have kidnapped them?' he asked, amused.

'Certainly not.'

'Then you are playing a game of hide-and-seek, perhaps?'

Jocelyn clenched her hands. 'This is not a *game*. It is imperative that I get these children out of sight.'

He looked quickly at her, then led his horse forward. 'Very well. You were making for that narrow path between the trees?'

'Yes. Paul, run ahead.'

They had just gained the shelter of the lane when Jocelyn realised that the unseen vehicle was taking the Honiton road, away from them. Relieved, she turned to Adam.

'I have a reason for desiring secrecy.'

'Am I to be enlightened, or is it confidential?'

She hesitated; then decided that it would be better to tell him the truth than that he should put his own construction on her behaviour. When she explained that the children were her sister's, he looked puzzled.

'But I understood from talk I heard at the inn where I am lodging that your sister had . . .'

'Eloped? That is true. It is a long story.'

'And one that does not concern me,' he said lightly. 'But if I can assist you in any way, I am at your service.'

She smiled at him gratefully. 'I want to get the children to a cottage on the western cliff, just above the stile where we first met. They can be looked after there by our old nurse until such time as my grandfather can be persuaded to have them.'

'And you are taking them down by this path so that they will not be recognised, is that it?'

'Yes,' she answered, relieved that he understood. 'I did not expect the little girls, only Paul. Had I known that they were coming as well, I should have brought Martha with me to meet them. In the circumstances, I shall be very glad of your help.'

'Lead the way then, Miss Harmer,' he said cheerfully, 'though it would appear we are about to enter an impenetrable jungle.'

'It is a path the smugglers use,' Jocelyn told him incautiously, as she walked ahead.

'Indeed? I had not guessed this peaceful valley contained so unlawful a community. There's no need to look so alarmed. My sympathies are entirely with the free-traders.'

'Take care to whom you say that. Galliards has long been suspected as a hiding-place for contraband. Some people say that the story of Sir John Peverell's ghost is kept alive to prevent strangers going too near.'

'In that case, I shall keep my eyes open for the chance of finding a keg or two of brandy concealed under my barn floor or in the stables. I'faith, it seems as if life at Penscombe will prove a deal more lively than expected.'

The lane became too narrow for a horse. Adam tethered the animal and handing the baby to Jocelyn, hoisted Isabella to his shoulders. As they set off again, the baby started to cry.

Paul said gravely, 'If you carry her over your shoulder, ma'am, she'll probably stop.'

Acutely embarrassed, Jocelyn did as he suggested.

Sarah immediately became interested in watching her sister who was treating Adam as if he were a horse.

'You'll soon learn, Miss Harmer,' Adam said cheerfully. 'Small children are demanding creatures, but I derive much enjoyment from their company. It is part of the pleasure of homecoming after a voyage, to be greeted with such enthusiasm by my nephews and nieces, though I dare swear some of the warmth of their welcome is due to anticipation of the presents I bring them.'

'Are you not rather young to own a merchant fleet?' Jocelyn asked.

He answered with pride. 'One of the youngest owners. My father died two years ago. As the only boy amongst six girls, I took over his ships. I first sailed with him when I was seven years old. When I returned home, I could scarcely wait to shock my sisters with a string of oaths which must have wellnigh scorched their ears.' His laughter sounded unnaturally loud in the enclosed lane. 'I was soundly thrashed, of course, when my father heard of it. Paul, you had better give me that portmanteau, it appears to be weighing you down.'

The boy straightened and thrust out his chin. 'I can manage, thank you, sir.'

It became increasingly clear to Jocelyn that she could not have managed, without Adam's help, to take the children down to Martha's cottage by this path. It was much rougher and steeper than she remembered. She had forgotten that the stepping-stones were apt to tilt alarmingly and that in parts, where the trees met overhead, it was dark enough to frighten children. When, eventually, they reached the path up the cliff, it assumed the aspect of a mountain track. Sarah's weight seemed out of all proportion to her size and she was crying persistently now—from hunger, Adam judged. Isabella grew tired of riding on his shoulders, but when he set her down she walked only a few yards before she demanded to be carried again. Twice Paul stumbled, and dropped the portmanteau. When Adam picked it up, the boy raised no objection. He had readily answered Adam's questions about Plymouth and told them how he had earned money by running errands, and helping at the blacksmith's and corn chandler's. But now he grew silent.

Jocelyn took hold of his hand as they started up the hillside. 'It is not far now. I expect Martha will have some hot soup ready for you.'

He made no response. His face was pale and set, and she could see that every step was an effort. Adam caught up with them.

'Come along, lad. Let me give you a pick-a-back.'

Paul straightened. 'No, thank you, sir. It is kind of you. But I am not a *girl*.'

Adam exchanged glances with Jocelyn.

'I have an idea,' he announced cheerfully. 'We will sing sea-shanties—oh, very proper ones, Miss Harmer, I assure you.'

He was still singing, in a pleasant tenor voice, as they trooped up the path to Martha's cottage. She was standing at the door, eyes wide with astonishment.

Jocelyn said hastily, 'Paul brought his sisters with him, Martha.'

Silently the old woman stared at the three children, then at Adam.

'This gentleman is Captain Peverell,' Jocelyn explained. 'He very kindly came to my assistance.'

Martha bobbed a curtsey, but still she seemed too stupefied to speak. Jocelyn felt Paul stiffen. He pressed himself against her. She saw that the anxiety had returned to his face.

She said urgently, 'I know it is a lot to ask of you, Martha, but if you *could* take them, just for tonight.'

Martha came suddenly to life. Her face lit up and she

held out her arms in a gesture which embraced the whole group.

'Of course I'll take them, ma'am, no doubt of that! What a fine surprise! Three children, instead of one!'

Ten minutes later Martha was seated at the table, the baby on her lap. Beside her, Isabella gulped down vegetable broth with a concentration which reminded Jocelyn of her grandfather. Seeing how small the room was, Adam had told Jocelyn that he would wait outside for her now that the old nurse had taken charge of the children.

Jocelyn looked with concern at Paul. He could scarcely keep his eyes open and it seemed too much effort for him to raise the spoon to his mouth.

'He'd best get to bed,' Martha said. 'Food will do him no good when he's as tired as that.'

'Where is he sleeping?' Jocelyn asked.

'I've made up a straw mattress and laid it on the oak chest in my bedroom. I'll have the two little girls in my own bed for tonight.'

'Shall I take him in?'

'I'd be glad if you would.' Martha looked from Jocelyn to the boy. 'He takes after you. But this little girl is the image of Miss Rosamund.' She glanced at Isabella, still happily absorbed in her supper.

Jocelyn put a hand on Paul's shoulder. 'Come with me and I will put you to bed.'

Sleepy as he was, he stood up straight and held his head high. 'I can put myself to bed, ma'am.'

Jocelyn exchanged smiles with Martha over the boy's head. She led him into the tiny bedroom which gave off the living-room. Despite his show of independence, he made no objection when she helped him to undress. But when she pulled down the blanket and would have lifted him into bed, he shook his head.

'I haven't said my prayers.'

He dropped to his knees. With an obvious effort at concentration, he muttered a series of prayers which Jocelyn recalled Martha teaching her and Rosamund in childhood. Then he added an impromptu one of his own.

'Please God, make Mama better, though I don't really think You can.'

Tears welled into Jocelyn's eyes. Quickly she brushed them away as Paul stood up. He climbed wearily on to the makeshift bed. Dressed only in his shirt he looked small and thin. Jocelyn, tucking him in, felt a tenderness which was akin to pain, and she had to stop herself from crying as she smoothed the dark hair away from his eyes and bent to kiss him goodnight. But he would not have seen her tears. For he was already asleep.

In the living-room, Martha looked at her with troubled eyes. 'You'd best get back now, Miss Jocelyn, or you'll be in trouble with Mr. Harmer.'

'But can you manage?'

'Of course. 'Tis wonderful to have little ones to look after again. If Mr. Harmer does agree to take them in, maybe I'll be needed back at Penn Barton,' she added wistfully. 'In the meantime, don't you fret yourself, ma'am.'

Jocelyn was just leaving as Martha asked, 'Who did you say the gentleman is who came with you? I don't recall setting eyes on him afore.'

'Captain Peverell. He has come to take over Galliards.'

The old woman gaped at her. 'Oh, my dear!' she exclaimed in dismay. 'If it ever came to your grandfather's ears . . .'

'I know,' Jocelyn said gravely. 'But I am sure I can trust Captain Peverell to respect my confidence. I had met him twice before. He is a very kind man.'

Martha nodded in agreement. 'And a fine, upstanding one, too, and with laughter in his eyes. But 'twill not do for you to become too friendly with him, Miss Jocelyn.'

'Do you not think I realise that?' Jocelyn asked bitterly. 'For myself, I would have been prepared to risk grand-father's anger, but now—now there are these children to be considered.'

'Aye,' Martha said sadly. ' 'Twill be a hard enough task to persuade Mr. Harmer to take them in, without you upsetting him by seeking the company of anyone bearing the name of Peverell.'

It was almost dark when Jocelyn reached home. Candle-light showed faintly through the cracks in the window shutters of her grandfather's bedroom, which must mean that the doctor had left and her grandfather retired un-usually early. She let herself in by the side door and sought Polly in the kitchen.

At sight of her mistress, the maid almost dropped the steaming kettle she was lifting from the range.

'Oh, ma'am, thanks be you'm back! There's been such a rumpus here.'

'Why, what has happened?'

'The master got into a rage and went so red in the face you'd have thought he must have burst! Us had to carry un up to bed, and the doctor has bled un, and . . .'

'When did this happen?' Jocelyn asked in dismay.

'About an hour since. Cook has the vapours and has taken herself off to her room, and Maisie's no more use than . . .'

Jocelyn cut her short. 'I will go up at once.'

Polly paused as she poured hot water into a copper jug. 'If I were you, ma'am, I'd bide downstairs and let the doctor come to you. When the master sees you, 'tis likely he'll work himself up again, which will not do him nor you a mite o' gude.'

Jocelyn hesitated. 'Very well. Tell Doctor Marsh I will see him in the library, as soon as I have tidied my-self.'

A big, thickset man, he came heavily into the room. His wig was askew, there was blood on his shirt.

Jocelyn asked anxiously, 'Is Grandfather very ill?'

'He will live,' the doctor answered laconically, and looked pointedly at the decanter of port on a side table.

'I am sure Grandfather would wish you to help yourself,' Jocelyn said. 'Then, I pray you, tell me what happened.'

Doctor Marsh poured himself a generous glass of port and held up the decanter to see how much was left. He settled himself in a chair before the fire, stretched out his legs and yawned.

'The old scoundrel had an attack of apoplexy. You know well enough what rages he gets into.'

'What caused it? Did he discover I was out for longer than I intended?'

He eyed her over the rim of his glass. 'No, that wasn't the cause. Though I dare say if he'd learned the *reason* for your long absence, it would have put him in more of a pet, eh? After all, 'tis late in the evening to be gathering primroses.'

Jocelyn ignored the implication. 'I am waiting for an explanation,' she said coldly.

The doctor sipped his port, refusing to be hurried. 'You never did take kindly to a bit of teasing, did you? But I'll wager you're not as innocent as you pretend. Oh, very well, if you're determined to be so solemn! Old Nathaniel's choler was due to what's happening across the valley, at the house with the fancy name.'

'Galliards, do you mean? Captain Peverell's house?'

'That's the one. Your grandfather complained that he couldn't concentrate on his game because of the hammering and banging, though I'll swear I never heard a sound. Then he insisted on telling me that old story of how his great-grandfather hunted down Sir John Peverell, and . . .'

'Yes, yes,' she broke in. 'I know it only too well. And then?'

The doctor drained his glass. With some reluctance, since she knew his weakness for wine, she picked up the decanter.

Watching her, he said, 'Fill it right up, if you please. I've deserved a full measure, I can assure you. Dealing with that old devil is as difficult as controlling an inmate of Bedlam.' He yawned widely; then, at Jocelyn's prompting, reluctantly continued telling what had happened. 'He banged his fist on the table and upset the chess-board—just as I saw a chance of winning, too— and went on muttering about the damned Cavaliers who had returned to Penscombe to plague him. I tried to reason with him, but 'twas useless. He sent for the maid to fetch his coat and hat, saying he was going over to Galliards to teach the Peverell fellow a lesson. Then he . . . But there's no need to go into details, Miss Harmer, they're not very pleasant hearing for a lady. At any rate, I considered it necessary to bleed him, and now he's lying as peaceful as a baby. But . . .' He raised a thick finger, 'I must warn you, he'll need to be kept very quiet. Any kind of shock or upset could have serious consequences.'

His eyes narrowed and he rubbed a hand thoughtfully over his stubby chin. 'Of course you'd scarcely be overcome with grief, would you, if . . . ?'

Jocelyn drew herself up. 'My feelings are not your concern, Doctor Marsh. In any case, they would in no way influence my duty towards my grandfather.'

The doctor pulled a face. 'You take a deal of pleasure in putting me in my place, don't you?' He drained his glass and looked at her bodly. 'You're a damned handsome woman, though there are times when you choose to look like a Puritan. I suppose you inherited that streak from the Roundhead ancestor your grandfather is always talking about. One thing's certain, though. There was none of the Puritan in your sister. I'll wager she didn't take walks for the sake of her health, and I'd surmise she didn't stay long with the fellow she ran off with. She'll have had a dozen lovers by now, and good luck to her, I say!'

Jocelyn bit back the retort she was tempted to make. To defend Rosamund's character would reveal too much.

The doctor rose and stretched. ''Tis obvious you're wanting to see the back of me. I'll come tomorrow, before church. Keep the old devil quiet, though I don't envy you your task.'

In the hall, picking up his hat, he said, 'You've a poor opinion of me, haven't you, Miss Harmer?'

Jocelyn regarded him levelly. 'I have the greatest respect for your skill as a physician. I know well enough that there are many people alive in this parish who would have died but for your care.'

He grunted. 'Maybe, maybe. But a man needs more from a woman than that. If you'd known me in London, when I was younger, before that virago I married drove me to the bottle . . .'

'Doctor Marsh, your wife has been dead over five years. Yet still . . .'

'I drink too much?' He put on his hat, sighing heavily. 'Yes, you're right. Once you give way to a weakness, it takes a hold on you. But you'd not understand that, would you? For you've no weaknesses, it seems. Sometimes I think you're too good to be true. And when you act in such a damned superior manner towards me, I'd give my eyes to discover a flaw and be able to take you down a peg or two. But I don't suppose I ever shall.'

3

In the morning, Jocelyn ordered the garden boy to lay straw in the lane, so that her grandfather would not be disturbed by the heavy wheels of the farm wagons. The shutters in his bedroom were opened only enough to let in some light. This being Sunday, there would be no work carried out at Galliards and, to Jocelyn's relief, word had come from Thomas Creedy that he had caught a chill and was keeping to his house.

Nathaniel lay in the four-poster bed, looking small and frail, his face almost as white as his tasselled nightcap. But his eyes were as alert as ever and his voice quite strong enough to find fault, from the manner in which Jocelyn arranged his pillows to the thinness of the gruel cook had prepared.

Even without the doctor's warning, Jocelyn soon realised that in these changed circumstances it would be impossible to raise the subject of Rosamund's children. She was sure that Martha would be willing to keep them for the present, but she could not be expected to shelter and feed three children on the pittance Jocelyn had, with difficulty, secured for her.

The only solution seemed to be to borrow from the housekeeping allowance. With an invalid on a restricted diet, it should surely prove possible, though how she would balance her accounts when her grandfather was well enough to scrutinise them, Jocelyn could not imagine.

She had no chance to go down to Martha on Sunday. On Monday morning she woke to hear rain beating against her windows. It continued all morning, and she wondered how Martha was managing with three children cooped up in her tiny cottage. Again, she found it impossible to escape from the house. The invalid's demands were endless. He wanted the shutters opened wider, then he wanted them closed. He wanted to be propped up, and five minutes later, to lie down. Jocelyn read to him, sat beside the bed while he slept fitfully, and carried out all Doctor Marsh's instructions despite the old man's protests.

She went to bed that night more exhausted than if she had walked twenty miles, yet so disturbed in her mind that sleep would not come for a long time. Apart from her anxiety over the children, her thoughts continually returned to Rosamund. Was she still alive? If so, who was looking after her? Since she did not even know Rosamund's address there seemed no way in which Jocelyn could help her sister.

She had tried to discover it from Paul. Adam, too, had questioned the boy closely, saying that he knew Plymouth well, having sailed from the port many times. But even he could not identify the actual street in which Rosamund had found lodgings after her husband's death.

Adam had been silent and thoughtful as he and Jocelyn walked down the cliff path in the dusk after seeing the children settled at Martha's. As they parted by the little bridge over the stream he had told her that he would help her in any way he could with the children, but that he was going away for a few days. He did not say where, or offer any reason for his journey. She supposed it was on some matter connected with the alterations to his house. In any case, Adam Peverell's affairs could be no concern of hers and, although she was sincerely grateful for his kindness, she felt a certain relief that she need not run the risk of meeting him. For the children's sake, she must do all she could to placate her grandfather, not deliberately flout his orders.

By Tuesday, Jocelyn felt she could no longer leave Martha to manage alone. When the doctor came, late in the afternoon, she told him that the invalid had been very restless and asked if he could give her grandfather a soothing medicine which would enable him to sleep more peacefully and for longer periods.

The doctor regarded her shrewdly. 'Is this request made for his sake or your own, Miss Harmer? I'm fully aware that you've been much put upon and could do with an outing, even if 'tis only one of those long walks you're so fond of taking—for the good of your health, of course.'

Ignoring his implication, she smiled at him. 'You are quite right, Doctor Marsh. These last few days have not been at all easy. I should enjoy a walk down to the sea.'

He took a small phial from his bag. 'Give him a pinch of this powder in some milk when he seems restless. But not more than three times in the day.' He twirled the phial in his strong fingers and regarded Jocelyn speculatively. 'I don't mind telling you, I'd think twice before giving this to some young women in your position.'

'Why? What is so different about my position?'

' 'Tis a damned unhappy one, I'd say. This powder could make it a deal easier. Your grandfather has had a long life and 'tis high time it came to an end, in my opinion. Then you'd be free, with a house of your own, money to spend, and no one to keep you tied like a dog on a chain.'

Jocelyn stared at him in dismay. 'You surely are not suggesting that I would deliberately end his life?'

'No, not you.' He handed her the phial and laughed shortly. 'There are times when I regard you as a prude, and too much guided by your conscience. But over this matter we are in accord. By the rules of my profession I am committed to preserve life, whatever my private opinion as to its worth. And you . . .' He picked up his bag and hat. 'However great your provocation, I'd stake my life it would never enter your head to take matters into your own hands, even by so simple a means as is contained in that phial.'

As soon as she was sure her grandfather was sleeping peacefully Jocelyn made a bundle of bedding and, hiding it beneath her cloak, set off for Martha's cottage by way of the wood and water meadows, avoiding the village.

As she came within sight of the cottage, she saw there was a man standing beside the gate. The setting sun was in her eyes and at first she did not recognise him. Then, with dismay mixed with pleasure, she saw that it was Adam Peverell.

'Do not scold me, Miss Harmer,' he greeted her. 'There is no one about to see us together, and if anyone should come this way I promise to disappear instantly.' He held out his hand. 'Let me take that bundle. As you came up the path, I had the disconcerting impression that you had grown suddenly very fat. What is in it? Contraband?'

'Nothing so dangerous. It is just bedding for the children.'

Despite her fear of discovery, she felt her spirits rise. In this man's presence her problems appeared less insurmountable, her burden of anxiety lifted a little.

'You have been visiting the children?' she asked. 'How are they?'

'Very well, and being cared for splendidly. She is a good soul, your Martha, and obviously devoted to you.'

'Does she know why I have not been able to come down before?'

'Yes. The news of your grandfather's illness has spread

around the village. It makes matters more difficult for you, I surmise.'

'That is true,' she said, and could not keep the weariness from her voice. 'He is difficult enough when he is well. Now . . .'

Adam nodded understandingly. 'Miss Harmer, there is something I must tell you. You may recall that I mentioned I was going away for a few days. I went, in fact, to Plymouth.'

She was surprised that he should speak of his journey now, when previously he had seemed so loath to do so.

She asked, out of courtesy, 'You had a ship coming into port, perhaps?'

'No, not yet. In fact my visit had nothing to do with my own affairs. I went to find your sister.'

She drew in her breath.

'It was not difficult,' he went on. 'Though Paul did not know the actual street, he gave me sufficient clues.' He put down the bundle of bedding. 'I am afraid I have not brought you good news.'

'Rosamund is—dead?'

'She died on Sunday night. I was with her.'

'*You?*'

'When I found her, she was very weak but quite lucid. She had remembered her two little girls and was distressed and anxious about them. I assured her that all her children were being cared for by you and her former nurse. After that, she was a great deal calmer, and slept. When she woke, she tried to send some message of gratitude to you, but . . . I have been present at many deaths, Miss Harmer. I do assure you, your sister's was without pain. She just—drifted away.'

Jocelyn bit hard on her finger, quite unable to speak. She turned away, trying to hold back her tears. Adam drew out his handkerchief and pressed it into her hand, then went to stand at the cliff edge, staring out to sea.

After a few minutes, when she had regained control of her feelings, Jocelyn went to him.

'Captain Peverell, you have been so very kind. There are no words sufficient to express my gratitude.'

'Then do not even attempt it,' he said lightly. 'There is one other matter on which I can give you reassurance. I was able to make suitable arrangements . . .'

'Arrangements?' she repeated, not understanding.

'For the—burial,' he explained with reluctance. 'It was, I think, carried out as you would have wished.'

'But Rosamund was penniless!' she exclaimed. 'Or so she wrote.'

'Yes, that was unfortunately true.'

'Then how . . . ?' She stared at him. He looked embarrassed and would not meet her eyes. 'Do you mean to say that *you* paid for Rosamund's burial? Why should you do that? You had not even met her.'

He took hold of her hand. 'I have sisters. If one of them met with similar misfortune, I should like to think there might be someone, even a stranger, who was able and willing to help.'

The tears welled again into Jocelyn's eyes. Helplessly she shook her head, unable to express what she felt. She could only hope that by the pressure of her fingers, he would understand.

'I have not told the children,' he said. 'Paul will take it hardest. Isabella is a deal more resilient than her delicate appearance would lead one to suppose.'

'I think you are right. She is so like her mother. But Paul . . . Poor little boy. He has endured so much already. And I can do so little for him.'

Adam said thoughtfully, 'If he shows any leaning towards the sea . . . But that is jumping ahead. Shall I send him to you so that you can tell him out here, alone?'

'If you please. Though I shall not know how to do so.

As I told you, I have no knowledge of children.'

He picked up the bundle of bedding. 'You do not need knowledge, only instinct. Every woman worthy of the name has the instinct to comfort those in need. It is as simple as that.'

She waited by the gate, finding it almost impossible to realise that her pretty, wayward sister was now lying in her grace, at twenty-seven.

The boy's steps dragged as he came towards her, and he hung his head.

Jocelyn said awkwardly, 'Captain Peverell has told you . . . ?'

'That you wanted to speak to me.' Paul raised his head and looked into her eyes. 'It's about Mama, isn't it? Is she dead?'

Jocelyn hesitated, then answered frankly, 'Yes, Paul. It happened on Sunday.'

Frowning, he clenched his hands. A spot of blood showed on his lower lip where he was biting it hard. Jocelyn held out her arms. He made as if to turn away. Then he flung himself at her and burrowed his head into her cloak.

She held him close, letting him sob out his grief. When he grew quieter, she said gently, 'Captain Peverell told your mother that you had brought your sisters safely to me. That made her happy, Paul.'

He nodded, sniffing. Jocelyn handed him Adam's handkerchief.

'What will happen now?' he asked. 'Will we stay with Martha?'

'For a little while. Your great-grandfather, with whom I live, is very ill. It is not possibe, at present, to have you there. Later, perhaps . . .'

She felt him shiver. The sun had gone down and the breeze off the sea was chill. She drew her cloak around him.

'Come, dear, let us go back to the cottage.'

The door, as usual, was open. A fire of driftwood burned brightly in the range. Adam sat in the rocking-chair with Isabella on his lap. Firelight shone on his bent head, enhancing the warm colouring of his hair. He was telling the little girl a story about a pony which had escaped from its stable. In the bedroom, Martha was crooning to the baby.

Jocelyn stood in the doorway, Paul clinging to her hand. The scene took on a strange familiarity. It was as if she was coming home, as if it was the most natural thing in the world that she should be here, with these children and this man, none of whom she had even met a week ago.

Then Adam shifted his position and a leaping flame illumined the ring on his right hand, the ring she had noticed when she had first seen him. It was a heavy gold signet ring, bearing the crest of the Peverells; the crest of the 'damned Cavaliers' towards whom her grandfather's hatred was so overwhelming that it had almost caused his death.

Her illusion ended abruptly. Even were she not tied by a marriage contract, Adam Peverell would be the last man in the world with whom she would be allowed to associate. He had proved himself a friend when she had been much in need of one. Now that friendship must end. If it continued, and word should reach her grandfather, the consequences might prove disastrous.

On her return to Penn Barton Jocelyn found, to her relief, that the invalid was still sleeping. He woke half an hour later and, after some persuasion, took some chicken broth. Then he lay back against the pillows with his eyes closed. His skin appeared so thin it was almost transparent, and the bones of his aquiline nose stood out sharply.

Despite the doctor's favourable report that afternoon, Jocelyn thought her grandfather was weaker. The fact that he showed an aversion to food, which usually he so enjoyed, seemed to her significant. For the first time, she faced the possibility that he might not recover. In that case, what would happen to Rosamund's children? She realised that she would be forced to confide in Thomas Creedy and ask his help. That prospect was not one she relished.

Through the open doorway of the bedroom, she heard one of the servants cross the hall and open the dining-room door. There was an odd, slithering sound, then a crash which brought Jocelyn to her feet. Nathaniel's eyes opened wide.

'What was that?' he demanded.

'I don't know. I will go and see.'

'It's those damned Cavaliers. There's no peace since they came back, no peace at all. They're always at their hammering. I'll burn down their house, that I will. Just wait until . . .'

Jocelyn pressed him gently back against the pillows. 'Lie still, Grandfather. It was probably only Polly banging a door.'

Fervently she hoped it *was* only that. There had been a maid once, hard-working and willing, who had dropped a tureen of soup which spilled over Nathaniel's legs. He had instantly dismissed her. Neither tears, nor Jocelyn's pleading, had saved the unfortunate girl from being packed off, penniless, that very night.

Jocelyn went quickly from the room, closing the door behind her. Looking over the banisters, she saw Polly in the hall. The maid was staring up the stairs, her hands pressed to her mouth.

Jocelyn called down quietly, 'What is it? What have you done?'

The girl shook her head. 'I've not done nothing, ma'am.

Look! See for yourself what's happened.'

Jocelyn went swiftly down to the first landing. On the stairs a portrait lay face downwards, its frame chipped and splintered. She knew, even before she glanced up at the wall, which portrait it was.

Polly said, in an awed voice, 'It means a death, ma'am, for sure, when a picture falls. Everyone knows that.'

Jocelyn ran her tongue over her dry lips. She made an effort to keep her voice steady.

'Put it in the dining-room, for the time being. I must go back to Grandfather.'

'Will you tell him, ma'am?'

Jocelyn did not answer. She cast another glance at the bare patch on the wall, then returned slowly upstairs. With her hand on the latch of the bedroom door, she paused, then resolutely lifted it and went in.

Nathaniel's fingers, gripping the quilt, reminded Jocelyn of birds' claws. His dark eyes glared at her as she approached the bed.

'What was it?' he demanded. 'If that clumsy girl has broken anything, she can leave this house at once. I'll not tolerate carelessness.'

Until that moment, Jocelyn had been undecided. Now, she said calmly, 'Nobody has broken anything, Grandfather. A portrait fell from the landing wall.'

'What?'

He shot up in bed, the tassel of his nightcap jerking forward. His eyes were wide open. His jaw sagged. He drew a long, shuddering breath.

'I'm going to die! That's what it means.' His voice rose to a screech. 'No. No! Jocelyn, don't let me die!'

It was the first time Jocelyn had seen him afraid. Momentarily, she experienced a sense of triumph. He was in her power, as, for so long, she had been in his. If she chose, she could make him suffer now, as he had made so many others suffer.

She did not choose. Pity took over. She bent and laid her hand over his, which was shaking violently.

She spoke reassuringly. 'You need not be afraid. *You* are not going to die. The death has already taken place.'

He looked up at her, breathing hard. His dark eyes, under their shaggy eyebrows, searched her face.

'What d'you mean? Whose death?'

She said slowly, 'It was Rosamund's portrait which fell. It is Rosamund who has died.'

His eyes narrowed. It was evident he did not believe her.

'How can you know what has happened to . . . ? No, I won't even speak her name. I ordered you to have nothing to do with her. I told you that if she wrote, you were not to answer.'

'I have not done so,' she said, sadly. 'I could not do so, for I did not even know where she was. She wrote me that she was very ill. She died on Sunday.'

He sank back against the pillows. His breath was coming in quick, short gasps.

'My little Rosamund,' he murmured querulously. 'She went away and left me. Not a word to me, not a word. Naughty Rosamund, naughty girl.' He raised his hands, then dropped them in a helpless gesture. 'Poor little Rosamund. Dead. I'll never see her again.' He looked up at Jocelyn. His eyes had softened, his lower lip drooped. There was nothing fierce about him now.

Jocelyn made up her mind. 'She had three children, Grandfather.'

His eyes hardened. 'Bastards?'

'No. She was married very soon after leaving home. Her husband is dead, too.'

'*Three* children, you said?'

'Yes. A boy and two girls.'

A little colour was returning to his cheeks. His eyebrows were drawn down. Jocelyn could no longer see his eyes. She held her breath, hoping against hope that the humanity she had just seen on his face would prompt him to show some concern for the children.

He spoke almost to himself. 'So? There are three children, offspring of a strolling player and his doxy.'

'Grandfather!'

He glared at her. 'That's what she was. Married or unmarried, that's what she was. Sneaking out like an alley-cat to meet her lover. Running away from home, bringing shame on her parents, heartbreak . . .'

His voice tailed off. He was silent for a few moments. Then he sat straight up and it seemed that his strength had fully returned. He looked so wild that involuntarily Jocelyn stepped back. When he turned to her, his expression was as hard as ever. He spoke with deliberate harshness.

'You will go downstairs and take that portrait into the yard and burn it. You will never mention that girl's name again, never. D'you understand?'

Jocelyn did not move. Even now, with all the evidence before her, she would not bring herself to believe that he could be so callous. She made a last, desperate attempt to sway him.

'But the children, Grandfather. They are not to blame for . . .' She broke off, seeing, before he spoke, that it was hopeless.

'They should have been drowned at birth!' His voice rose, became shrill. 'Drowned, d'you hear? Like May kittens.'

Jocelyn shut her eyes. Clearly she could visualise Paul, standing small and vulnerable before her, saying beseechingly, 'I have brought my sisters, they are only little.'

He trusted her, sure of her ability to care for him and his sisters. But she was powerless against this inhuman, vindictive old man. What was it the doctor had said? ' 'Tis time his life came to an end . . .'

There was a heavy candlestick on the table beside the bed. She had only to reach out her hand . . .

She turned on her heel and rushed from the bedroom. Reaching her own room, she flung herself on the bed. She beat at the pillow with clenched fists, drawing long, sobbing breaths. Never in her life had she given way so completely to her feelings. But never had she faced a temptation so appalling.

For most of that night, Jocelyn lay awake, staring at the dark sky beyond her unshuttered windows. Faced with the certainty that she could not bring the children to Penn Barton, she realised that she must make other plans at once. She discarded one idea after another until finally she evolved a plan which seemed possible to carry out.

She would place the children with a decent, kind woman at some distance from the village. There she would keep them hidden, like a vixen with her young, until they were old enough to fend for themselves. Paul was already of an age to be apprenticed, if only she could raise the money.

Money, she soon realised, would be her main problem. She had none that she could call her own, save her dress allowance, and that was only just adequate. But her mother had left her a few good pieces of jewellery, and these she would have no compunction in selling for the purpose she had in mind. In the attic were some odd articles of china and brass and copper, of which Nathaniel was unaware. They would fetch a few guineas. Perhaps she herself could learn the art of lace-making and so, secretly, earn some money.

But she would need help. The doctor could certainly not be trusted to keep silent. The parson was old and very deaf, and nowadays his mind wandered. She wondered if she should confide in Thomas, but decided against it. For it was unlikely he would take part in any plans of which her grandfather disapproved, for fear of prejudicing his chance of eventually procuring her dowry.

There remained only one person whom she could wholly trust and of those willingness to help she had no doubt. She would have to seek assistance from Adam Peverell. If she was careful, there surely was little risk of their association reaching the ears of her grandfather while he was confined to his bedroom and forbidden any visitors.

In the morning she gave cook her instructions for the day and told Polly to sit with the invalid, adding that, should he ask for her, he should be told she had gone to Martha's to fetch goat's milk for him. Then she cut Rosamund's portrait from the shattered frame and hid it beneath her mattress, before taking the broken pieces of wood into the stable yard and ordering the garden-boy to burn them. At least she would be able to tell her grandfather truthfully that he would never see Rosamund's portrait again.

Tying her few pieces of jewellery in a handkerchief, she slipped them down the bodice of her gown. She had discovered a coat of her brother William's, a green coat with silver buckles, and some baby clothes which had been laid away for over twenty years in the lavender-scented chest in the night nursery. These she wrapped in a banket and hid beneath the cloak. Stealthily as a smuggler with contraband, she made her way down to the cliff.

There was a heavy swell on the sea. The pebbles rattled as the undertow of the waves sucked them down the beach. Gulls wheeled overhead, calling incessantly. There was no one in sight, not even a fisherman or a farm labourer, as Jocelyn went up the steep path and climbed over the stile.

A figure disappeared into the hedge a few yards from her. Startled, she drew back. She heard a loud whisper.

'It's me, Aunt Jocelyn.'

'Paul! You made me jump.'

He emerged from the hedge, his hair tousled. 'You said I was to make sure no one saw me. You didn't really see me, did you?'

'No, not properly. I thought you were an animal of some sort.'

'What sort?'

'One of Martha's goats, perhaps.'

'I could pretend to be a goat. Look, like this.'

He raised his two forefingers above his head, pawed the ground with one foot, and imitated the bleating of the old billy-goat.

Jocelyn burst out laughing. The boy, looking pleased, capered around her. She felt relieved that he could behave in so light-hearted a fashion. Until now, she had seen only anxiety and grief on his face.

'What are you doing down here?' she asked, when he paused for breath.

'Setting snares. Captain Peverell showed me how.'

'When was this?'

'Earlier this morning. He came with a rabbit for Martha to cook for our dinner, and he brought a little horse for Isabella that he'd carved out of wood. He's a very kind man, isn't he, ma'am?'

'Yes,' she agreed readily, 'the kindest I have ever met.'

She was disappointed that she had missed Adam for she could have handed him her jewellery to sell.

She pulled aside her cloak. 'Look what I have brought you.'

Delightedly, the boy took the coat from her. 'Papa had a coat the same colour as this, once. It was when we were in Bristol and he had some money to spare. He bought Mama a new gown, too, a pink one with frills.'

He put on the coat and buttoned it up. Then he squared his shoulders and strutted up and down before Jocelyn, assuming a dandified air. For the first time, she was reminded that his father had been an actor.

'You look very smart,' she told him. 'I will try and find you some breeches to match.'

His eyes shone. 'Then I shall look really grown-up. Thank you, Aunt Jocelyn. Can we go and show my coat to Martha?'

'Of course. Tell me, what else have you been doing this morning?'

'I fetched water from the stream, and did some digging in the garden. Then Captain Peverell came.' He glanced up at her. 'Will I be able to go to sea with him one day?'

'Is that what you would like to do?'

'I think so. There were lots of ships at Plymouth and Bristol. It was exciting, watching them unload their cargoes, and getting ready to sail away again.'

As Adam will sail away again one day, Jocelyn thought, and felt suddenly cold despite her cloak.

'Can you read and write, Paul?' she asked.

He nodded eagerly. 'Papa taught me, and to do sums. I can do lots of things, ma'am.'

She gave his shoulder an affectionate squeeze and smiled down at him.

When they reached the cottage, Jocelyn found Martha sitting on a low chair before the fire, attending to the baby. She looked up happily as Jocelyn greeted her.

' 'Tis a long time since I did this, ma'am. But babies don't alter their ways.'

Paul stood proudly before her. 'See my coat, Martha. Aunt Jocelyn just gave it to me.'

'And a very fine young gentleman you look in it.'

Martha's eyes clouded with memory. 'I recall the day Master William first wore that coat. He was . . .' She stopped, shaking her head. 'But I'll not waste my breath on past misfortunes. 'Tis the future we've to be concerned with now, Miss Jocelyn.'

'You are right,' Jocelyn agreed, taking off her cloak. 'I have been making plans. I need your help, Martha, and Captain Peverell's.'

'You know I'll do anything in my power. As to Captain Peverell, you need have no doubts on that score. I never knew a man concern himself so over young children. Though I doubt 'tis only the children as have taken his fancy.' She pulled down Sarah's dress. 'There now, my lamb, that's more comfortable, isn't it? I'll just get rid of these soiled clothes, ma'am, then I'll be back to hear these plans of yours.'

The baby crawled underneath the table, bent on picking up some chicken feathers. Paul took off his coat and laid it carefully over the back of the rocking-chair.

'Where is Isabella?' Jocelyn asked.

'She went to look at the goats. They're the next best thing to horses.'

'Then it is to be hoped she will not attempt to ride them. Paul, I think you had better go and see . . .'

'Oh, very well,' he said, sighing heavily. 'But I'm *always* keeping Isabella out of trouble.' He turned at the door and added, in a tone of awe, 'Captain Peverell told me has has six sisters. I expect he was very glad to go to sea.'

Jocelyn was still laughing when Martha returned. Her old nurse glanced at her approvingly.

'That's how I like to hear you, Miss Jocelyn. Have you seen the sea-chest Captain Peverell brought?'

'A *sea-chest*. Whatever for?'

'To be used as a cradle for the baby. 'Tis deep enough

for her not to climb out of, and he's coming later today to remove the lid.'

Jocelyn knelt on the floor. The chest was of polished teak, with brass fastenings. She lifted the domed lid, then exclaimed in surprise.

'It is full of Captain Peverell's things.'

'He said I was to empty it. He brought the chest down from the inn where he's lodging, and he thought his belongings might be safer here than at Galliards while the house is still empty.'

Jocelyn lifted out some seaman's clothes, then a carefully wrapped packet. Her curiosity got the better of her and she pulled aside the wrapping.

'Oh, what beautiful lace! I've never seen patterns like this in any of the pillow-lace made by the village women. It must be French.'

Martha peered over her shoulder. 'That will have cost him a good few guineas, I'm thinking.'

Jocelyn delved again into the chest and brought out a heavy Bible wrapped in a fine silk handkerchief. On the fly-leaf was the Peverell family tree.

Jocelyn studied it with interest, tracing Adam's ancestry. 'I suppose I should not be looking at this,' she confessed, 'but . . . Oh!'

'What is it?' Martha asked.

Jocelyn put her finger under one of the entries. 'Look, there.'

'You know I can't read, Miss Jocelyn. What does it say?'

Jocelyn frowned. 'It says, "This Bible belonged to Sir John Peverell of Galliards, Penscombe in the county of Devon, who was killed while serving his King, by Edmund Harmer of Penn Barton Manor, in the same parish." ' She sat back on her heels. 'Captain Peverell must have been aware of the feud between our families, before I mentioned it.'

'Even if he was, you can't say but what he's doing his best to put an end to it. And about time, too.'

Jocelyn, returning to the chest, discovered half a dozen more handkerchiefs. They were of very fine silk and delicately worked in an Eastern design. She ran them gently through her fingers.

'How very lovely they are. Martha, you had better put these things away carefully. If Isabella or the baby should get hold of them, they may get damaged.' She folded one of the blankets she had brought and laid it in the bottom of the chest. 'It will make a most comfortable cot. Oh, Martha, last night I came nearer to despair than ever before. This morning, thanks to you and Captain Peverell, everything I have been planning seems possible.'

Martha smiled at her affectionately. 'When you're bent on protecting others, I've never known anything defeat you. 'Tis where your own happiness is concerned that your conscience gives you so much trouble. 'Tis then that I most fear for you, my dear.'

Paul ran into the kitchen. 'I can't find Isabella *anywhere*. I've called and called, but she won't answer.'

'I told her not to go beyond the fence.' Martha said. 'She's a disobedient child, that one, just like her mother before her.'

She scooped up Sarah and dumped her in the sea-chest, tossing in Isabella's wooden horse.

'Is it safe?' Jocelyn asked. 'Are you sure the lid won't fall shut?'

Martha tried it. ' 'Tis too stiff, and she can't reach it. She's safe enough for the present.'

Together they searched around the cottage, behind the hen-house, peered into the wood-shed.

'We had better separate,' Jocelyn suggested. 'Martha, will you go down the hill? Paul, have a look in the copse.'

'She won't be there,' the boy assured her. 'Isabella doesn't like dark places.'

'It's not dark there, not like a wood.'

'*She'd* think it was,' he persisted.

'Very well,' Jocelyn conceded. 'Come with me, up the hill.'

Jocelyn hoped fervently that Isabella had not gone that way, for there was no path beyond the cottage. In the old days, so she had been told, smugglers had used this western cliff and hidden their contraband in the cottage, occupied then by one of their number. But a landslide, some years back, had broken away a great slice of cliff and left a pinnacle of chalk separated from the mainland. After that, it had proved useless for their purpose. Jocelyn had not been up here for years. Even her adventurous spirit was daunted by the thought of what could happen if one false step was taken.

Paul, running ahead, stopped abruptly. He pointed to a strip of material hanging on a gorse bush.

'That's Isabella's hair ribbon. She must have come this way.'

He shouted at the top of his voice. There was no reply. Some way above them something disappeared behind a bush.

'She's probably playing side-and-seek,' Paul said disgustedly. 'She *is* a nuisance, isn't she?'

'Perhaps she will take notice of me,' Jocelyn suggested.

But the only answer to her call was a faint giggle. Paul gave her a look which said clearly, 'Now you can see what I mean.'

Bunching her skirts, Jocelyn started up the hill again. The little girl darted from one gorse bush to another. Jocelyn gasped as she saw how near the child was to the edge of the cliff.

'Isabella, stay where you are,' she called urgently. She turned to Paul. 'Come round to the other side of me.'

'Why, Aunt Jocelyn?'

Fear lent sharpness to her voice. 'Do as I say, and don't ask questions.'

As they continued upwards, the boy saw the reason for her precaution.

In an awed voice he exclaimed, 'The cliff goes down and down! I didn't know the edge was so near.'

Jocelyn kept her eyes on the bush behind which Isabella was hiding. A few yards to the child's right, the edge of the landslip showed starkly white. But Isabella could not see it. At her height only gorse bushes and grass would be visible.

She danced up and down behind the bush. 'You can't catch me! You can't catch me!'

Jocelyn had an inspiration. 'No, we can't catch you, Isabella. But if you stay quite still and let us come and find you, you shall have a ride on Captain Peverell's horse.'

There was silence for a moment. Then the child asked, 'Is Captain Peril there?'

'Not yet. He will come soon.'

Isabella said doubtfully, 'He didn't let me ride his horse this morning. He just brought me a little wooden one. I can't ride that.'

'He was in too much of a hurry,' Jocelyn told her. 'When he comes again, he will have more time, and I will ask him.'

The little girl appeared hesitantly around the bush. 'Is that a promise?'

Jocelyn cautiously stepped forward a few paces. 'Yes, it is a promise. Come now, dear.' She held out her hand.

Isabella, suddenly making up her mind, began to run towards Jocelyn. A seagull swooped up over the cliff, checked at sight of humans, turned in its flight and glided out of sight.

Isabella checked, also. 'Pretty bird,' she exclaimed delightedly. 'Where has it gone?'

She started forward again in the direction the bird had taken, quite oblivious of the danger. Horrified, Jocelyn ran after her. The child turned, startled. Just behind her was the edge of the landslip and beyond, the stark white pinnacle of rock, rising straight out of the sea.

Jocelyn caught Isabella by the wrist and dragged her back. The ground moved beneath her feet. She pushed Isabella away, sending her sprawling on the grass.

The force she had used threw Jocelyn off balance and she fell. She began to slide, on her stomach, over the edge of the cliff. Desperately she grasped at the short grass, at stalks of furze, roots, anything which could save her. None of it held. She sought for a foot-hold. The loose chalky rock crumbled beneath her feet. She slithered helplessly down the face of the cliff, towards the beach far below.

Suddenly, her feet touched solid ground. She fell backwards, in a welter of stones and chalk dust. Something hit her between the shoulders. The breath was knocked out of her. The world went black.

When she recovered her senses, Jocelyn found that she was lying on her back, staring up at the sky. At first, everything seemed strangely calm and quiet. Then she became aware of gulls screaming overhead, of small stones pattering down the cliff, the sound of the sea. To her surprise, the rhythmic rise and fall of the waves on the beach seemed still a long way below her.

Cautiously, she turned her head from side to side. She saw that her fall had been broken by one of the small ridges left by the landslip. It was several feet wide, overgrown with furze and stunted hawthorn bushes.

She could hear Paul calling. But she had not the strength yet to make herself heard above the raucous screaming of the gulls. As she moved slightly, the pain in her back made her cry out. But she forced herself to sit up, and then to test every limb. She did not seem to have broken any bones. Her hands were bleeding profusely, her gown ripped, her eyes smarting from chalk dust. But, miraculously, she was alive, and not seriously injured.

The cries of the gulls lessened as some flew out to sea. Paul called again. Looking up, Jocelyn saw his head appear over the edge of the cliff.

'Get back,' she called urgently. 'Paul, get back from the edge.'

'I'm all right,' he shouted down. 'I'm on my stomach. It's quite firm here. Oh, Aunt Jocelyn . . .' His voice broke. 'I thought you'd be killed.'

It took all her strength to call up to him. 'Where is Isabella?'

'She's run back to Martha. She was frightened.' Paul's head disappeared.

'I've gone back a bit, Aunt Jocelyn. Can you still hear me?'

'Yes. Stay where you are. I'm going to try and stand up.'

She turned on to her knees and crawled carefully nearer to the face of the cliff. Stiffly, she rose to her feet, wincing at the pain in her back. The ridge ran a few yards to right and left. Beyond, there was a sheer drop to the beach. She was trapped, with no hope of climbing up the cliff, for there were no footholds, nothing for her to hold on to.

A wave of panic swept over her. She began to tremble. Then, resolutely, she talked aloud, just as she had done as a child when her own recklessness had landed her in a dangerous situation.

'Don't lose your head. There is no danger, if you stay still. You have only to wait until help comes. Paul will go for help.'

She called to him. 'Listen to me, carefully. Go back to Martha and tell her what has happened. Tell her I am not badly hurt but I cannot move from this ridge. Ask her to get someone with a rope. Do you understand?'

'Yes.' He repeated her instructions, and added eagerly, 'I'll run all the way.'

After he had gone, Jocelyn sat with her back against the cliff. She wiped away the worst of the blood and dirt from her cut hands on her petticoat.

After that, there was nothing she could do but wait. She wondered who would come to her rescue. Farmer Blakiston was the nearest. Whoever came, she realised with dismay, would ask questions. There would have to be an explanation of how she came to fall down the cliff. The children would be seen. All the fine plans she had made would be set at naught.

She felt suddenly cold, and terribly alone. Doubts crept into her mind. Suppose Paul should lose his way or venture too near the edge of the cliff? Suppose he should not tell Martha properly what had happened. After all, he was only nine.

Again, she took a grip of herself. She concentrated on watching the gulls, trying to distinguish one bird from another. Then she noticed a ship, far out at sea. She kept her gaze on it, speculating about its destination.

At last, above the gull's cries, she heard a human voice. She got to her feet, gasping as her bruised body rebelled against the effort. Steadying herself, she looked up.

A head appeared over the edge of the cliff. Against the blue sky, auburn hair showed plainly. She heard Adam's voice.

'Can you hear me?'

'Yes,' she called back, but her voice sounded so weak

she doubted if it would reach him.

'Stay quite still,' he shouted.

She pressed herself against the cliff, scarcely able to believe it was Adam who had come to her rescue. Yet it seemed inevitable. Whenever she needed him, he was there. She found herself wanting to cry, the relief was so great.

He called down again. 'Can you step across to that clump of hawthorns? The ground looks firm there.'

'Good,' he commented, as she did as he told her. 'Sit down and don't move. I'm coming down.'

She started to protest. 'You cannot . . .'

'I have my horse here, and a rope. If it's strong enough to restrain that fearsome billy-goat of Martha's, it'll take my weight. So stop arguing. It's a habit you're over-fond of.'

Jocelyn began to giggle. She was still laughing, a little hysterically, as Adam lowered himself down the cliff.

Kneeling beside her, he put an arm around her shoulders.

'Hush, now,' he said, as if he was talking to Sarah. 'I'm here with you. You're not alone any more.'

The tone of his voice was her undoing. The tears streamed down her cheeks and she buried her face against his shoulder. He took out his handkerchief and gently wiped her face and hands.

After a few minutes, she drew away from him and sat up. 'I am sorry. I am not usually given to such weakness.'

He looked at her with the half-amused expression which had grown so familiar. 'You are not usually, I trust, given to falling down cliffs.'

She laughed and this time it had a natural ring.

'That's better,' he said cheerfully. But there was concern in his eyes as he examined her hands. 'It is not going to be easy for you, holding to a rope. I must bandage them somehow.'

He tied his handkerchief around her left hand, then pulled off his cravat and wound it around the other.

'That is the best I can do. Now, listen. You must . . . you are not listening to me. What is the matter? Are you feeling faint?'

She shook her head.

Adam said insistently, 'Try to concentrate. I am . . .'

'My jewels,' she said dully. 'I have lost them.'

He looked at her anxiously, and again spoke as if to a child. 'I realise you have had a great shock, but . . .'

'The jewels must have dropped out as I fell,' she said, putting a hand to her torn bodice. 'They may be—anywhere. Oh please try to find them.'

'Yes, yes, later,' Adam said placatingly. 'But at this time of day you would scarcely have been wearing a valuable . . .'

"You don't understand. I've lost all the jewellery I possess. I was going to ask you to sell it for me, to help the children.'

She looked at him helplessly, and saw by his expression that he suspected her mind was deranged by her fall. Wearily she shook her head.

'I am not mad. It is a long story.'

'Which can wait,' he said firmly. 'The most important thing now is to get you up the cliff. First, I'm going to tie this rope around your waist.'

When he had done so, with a sailor's skill, he helped her to her feet, and led her to the base of the cliff.

'You must hold tightly to the rope, despite the pain in your hands. My horse will take your weight, but you must push with your feet to keep yourself away from the cliff." He raised his voice. 'Paul, are you ready?'

The boy's voice came down to them, shrill with excitement. 'Yes, sir, quite ready.'

'Good. Then go ahead. Slowly, mind, slowly.'

Jocelyn caught hold of the rope and braced her feet

against the cliff as she was lifted clear of the ground. Every muscle seemed stretched to its limit. The pain in her hands was excruciating. It took all her concentration to keep herself away from the rock face. Halfway up, a wave of panic almost overwhelmed her.

Adam called up to her. 'Keep going. You're doing splendidly. We'll make a sailor of you yet.'

The calmness in his voice steadied her. In a few minutes more, her head was level with the top of the cliff. She heard Paul's voice.

'Steady, boy, steady. Whoa, now.'

Jocelyn lay face downwards on the grass, at the end of her strength. She felt the rope being untied from her waist. Then she was raised up and Martha's arms were around her.

'Thank God you'm safe!' the old woman exclaimed, brokenly. 'I was so afraid for you, my dear, dear girl.'

Martha rocked her, crooning as if she was a child. Jocelyn would have liked to stay in Martha's arms, making no effort, her mind a blank. But Adam was still down the cliff.

She scrambled to her feet and called down to him.

'I am safely up. Shall I throw the rope down?'

'Yes. But take care my coat is still under it to stop it chafing. Tell Paul to lead the horse back to where I left him, and then wait until I tell him I'm ready.'

To Jocelyn, Adam's ascent seemed to take even longer than her own. She wondered if she should go to Paul's aid. But Adam had not told her to do so and despite his youth, the boy was managing perfectly. She watched the horse plodding steadily away from the cliff. She watched the rope, straining under Adam's weight, sliding up over his folded coat on the edge of the cliff.

At last his head came into view. A few seconds later he shouted to Paul to stop and leaped agilely on to level ground. Untying the rope from his waist, he looked anxiously at Jocelyn.

'Are you all right, Miss Harmer?' As she nodded, too relieved for the moment even to speak, he said warmly, 'You have immense courage. I will admit now, that I doubted if you would manage.'

'There be few things Miss Jocelyn can't manage,' Martha said stoutly. 'Always getting in and out of scrapes she was, as a child. But this time . . .' She shook her head and looked near to tears.

Jocelyn put an arm about the old woman's shoulders. 'It's all over, Martha. I'm safe, thanks to Captain Peverell, and Paul.'

The boy was coming towards her, coiling the rope. Adam clapped him on the shoulder.

'Well done, lad. No grown man could have done better. I'll sign you on as one of my crew any time you like.'

Paul's head was held high, his eyes very bright, as he patted the horse's neck. 'I saved Aunt Jocelyn's life, didn't I?' he asked proudly.

'Indeed you did,' Jocelyn answered warmly. 'I shall never forget that, Paul.'

Martha had recovered herself. 'We'd best get you to the cottage, Miss Jocelyn, and bathe those poor hands. And a cup of tea will do you good.' She turned to Adam. 'Will you be helping her down, sir?'

'Of course. Paul, can you lead my horse down the hill?'

The boy nodded eagerly, and set off, with Martha following. Before Jocelyn could guess his intention, Adam had lifted her in his arms.

'If you start to argue now,' he said, 'I shall drop you over the cliff again.'

The protest she had been about to make dissolved into helpless laughter. She forgot the pain in her back and hands. The fact that her gown was torn, her shoes scraped and her stockings ruined, seemed of little consequence. Now that the danger was over, she felt ridiculously light-hearted.

Adam looked at her appreciatively. 'I have already said you have great courage. Now I will tell you something else. Even with chalk dust on your nose and bits of furze in your hair, you are still a very beautiful woman.'

4

There was a horse tethered to the iron ring set in the wall beside the steps to Penn Barton. At first Jocelyn thought it was the doctor's; then she recognised it as the grey, with cropped mane and tail, which belonged to Thomas Creedy. She entered the house by the side door and, bidding Polly follow her, went up to her bedroom by the back stairs.

The maid gasped at her mistress's appearance. 'Why, ma'am, whatever . . . ?'

Jocelyn cut her short. 'I fell. That is all I can tell you. Help me to change my gown and pin up my hair.' As the maid started to undo the fastenings, Jocelyn asked, 'Where is Mr. Creedy?'

'With the master. He heard tell of Mr. Harmer's illness and decided to call and enquire after him.'

Jocelyn winced as Polly pulled off her gown. 'Gently, Polly. I have wrenched my back. Has Grandfather missed me?'

'He did ask for you, ma'am, so I told him what you said, about going for the goat's milk.'

"Oh, I had quite forgotten about that.' She looked down at her hands, now bandaged with clean linen by Martha. 'Nothing this morning has gone as I had planned.'

The maid eased off Jocelyn's torn stockings. ' 'Tis obvious you've had a bad fall, ma'am. Wouldn't it be better to go to bed with a hot brick at your feet and a compress on your back?'

Nothing would have pleased Jocelyn more. But it was

impossible, without inviting questions both from her grandfather and Thomas. When Polly had done, Jocelyn surveyed herself in the mirror.

'Rub a little rouge on my cheeks. I look as if I still have chalk dust over my face.'

She walked stiffly downstairs and into the drawing-room, to wait for Thomas. It was not long before he appeared, ushered in by Polly.

'I am sorry I was not here to receive you,' Jocelyn said as he stood before her, hand outstretched. 'You must excuse me,' she added, 'but as you see, I have had an accident.'

He still held his hand extended and did not seem to take in her words.

'To my hands,' she explained, showing them to him.

'Oh. Oh, I see. I am sorry.'

There was no concern in his voice, and he made no further comment, but sat down, his knees close together, and stared at the floor.

'You will take some wine?' Jocelyn asked. She motioned to Polly, hovering in the doorway, to wait on them.

'Thank you, yes,' Thomas said with the same abstracted air. 'Indeed, I shall be glad of some refreshment. I set out early this morning. It is a long ride from Honiton, as you know, and I scarcely anticipated being received in such . . .' He broke off abruptly as Polly handed him a glass of wine.

Jocelyn waited until the maid had left them. Then she said, 'You have doubtless found Grandfather a little —difficult.'

'Difficult! He was downright . . .' Thomas cleared his throat. 'I beg your pardon, Miss Jocelyn. But I've just had one of the most uncomfortable half-hours of my whole professional career. With all respect, ma'am, I have come to the conclusion that your grandfather must be a little deranged.'

Jocelyn was of the same opinion, but she was not going to admit it to the lawyer. She said carefully, "You must remember that he is very old and his illness . . .'

'Even so, the suggestions he put to me . . .'

Jocelyn sipped her wine. 'Do you wish to tell me about it?'

Thoughtfully, he rubbed a thin hand over his chin. His usual self-assurance and precise manner seemed to have deserted him.

He said eventually, 'Indeed, I consider it my duty to tell you. My duty to myself, that is, so that I may refute the implication Mr. Harmer put upon my visit this morning. Your grandfather had the effrontery'—his voice rose —'the *effrontery*, to suggest that I had not come to enquire about his health, but in the hope that . . . No, after all, I cannot bring myself to repeat his words.'

'Then perhaps I may help you out,' Jocelyn offered. She felt a certain amount of sympathy for the discomfited lawyer. 'He suggested, I surmise, that you had ridden over in the hope of finding him on his deathbed.'

Thomas's pale eyes widened. 'That is precisely what he said. To say that I was shocked, Miss Jocelyn . . .'

'I should have thought you had known Grandfather too long to be shocked by his outbursts. I dare say he went on to imply that you had no real concern about his health but were only waiting to get your hands on my dowry.'

Two spots of colour appeared in Thomas's cheeks. 'Those were his words exactly. To a man in my position, a man of—if I may be allowed to say so—the highest principles, it was most hurtful and uncalled for.'

But true, all the same, Jocelyn thought. She knew well enough that this cold, egotistical lawyer had no more affection for her grandfather than she had. Probably less, for until last night she had at least felt some pity towards the old man.

'Even that was not all,' Thomas went on. 'Having imputed, as I have already mentioned, an avaricious motive to my visit, he went on to make the most outrageous suggestions as to how I should proceed in a—a certain matter. To carry them out would be most prejudicial to my reputation. In fact, such a course would be entirely against the proper conduct of my profession.'

Jocelyn's attention began to stray. Her back was aching, her hands smarting. She longed to act on Polly's suggestion and lie down on her bed. Then, suddenly, at mention of a name, she jerked up her head.

'. . . Captain Peverell's title to Galliards,' Thomas was saying. 'The suggestion that I should falsify evidence, and fabricate doubts regarding the good faith of another member of my profession, is quite repugnant to me. I am no admirer of Samuel Cartwright, and as I believe I mentioned, I was surprised that a gentleman of Captain Peverell's standing should have gone to him for advice when I would have been most willing, most *willing* to deal with his affairs. Nevertheless, although I consider my own abilities greatly in excess of Mr. Cartwright's I have never had cause to question his integrity.'

Jocelyn sighed. If only he would come to the point . . .

'Am I to understand that is what Grandfather wishes you to do?' she asked.

'Exactly that.' Thomas pressed his thin lips together. 'He wishes me to suggest to Mr. Cartwright that he failed to peruse the deeds correctly and has now discovered a discrepancy which renders Captain Peverell's title to Galliards invalid. Your grandfather would, in his own words, "make it worth Cartwright's while".'

'But that is shameful, Mr. Creedy! I do not wonder that you were shocked at such a suggestion.'

Thomas inclined his head. 'I must thank you, Miss

Jocelyn, for the assurance contained in your words, although I did not think that you would entertain for a moment the idea that I would be influenced in the slightest degree by the question of money, either in this matter, or in my concern for Mr. Harmer. I will not deny that there have been times when certain law suits in which he has instructed me to act for him have been a little—delicate. They have been small matters, such as the diversion of a leat, the placing of a fence, possession of a cottage; a few cases of theft of firewood or hedge trimmings—small matters, as I have said, involving no person of higher status than a yeoman farmer. But to imagine that one could cross a man like Captain Peverell . . .'

Jocelyn rose and went to stand by the window, her back to Thomas. 'Yes,' she said, almost to herself, 'to cross a man like Captain Peverell would be quite a different matter.'

Across the valley, smoke was rising above the trees which hid Galliards from view from this angle. Faintly she could hear the sound of hammering. 'I have never known a man so concern himself with young children,' Martha had said of Adam. Yet the great-grandfather of these same children was now hatching up a scheme to dispossess him of his home.

She should have guessed something of the sort would happen. It was unlikely that her grandfather's antagonism towards the Peverells would confine itself to shaking his fist and cursing 'the damned Cavaliers'.

She turned to Thomas. 'I assume that you declined to act in any way against Captain Peverell.'

Thomas smoothed his cuffs. 'I—I would not use the words "in any way".' He gave his little dry cough. 'Naturally, I refused to employ methods which constitute unprofessional conduct. But there is no harm in making—certain enquiries . . .'

'About what? Surely you do not doubt that Captain Peverell is the rightful owner of the house?'

Thomas rubbed his chin. 'I have no reason to doubt it. There are—other matters which call for some little investigation.'

She went closer to him. 'What other matters?'

Thomas gave her his frosty smile. 'Ah, Miss Jocelyn, you must not ask me that.'

'But I *am* asking you,' Jocelyn said urgently. 'What is there to investigate? What harm can you do to Captain Peverell? And why should you wish to harm him?'

Thomas regarded her as if she was an over-excited child. 'I will answer all your questions in turn,' he said with unctuous patience, and began to tick them off on his fingers. 'First, there are certain activities at Galliards to be investigated. Second, I do not like the word "harm" in this context. If Captain Peverell has contravened the law, he must be brought to court. As to why I should wish to act in this matter, there are two reasons. One, I am Mr. Harmer's lawyer and therefore it is my duty to carry out his wishes, provided they do not involve me in unprofessional conduct. Second, there is a personal consideration involved. As you are probably aware, I have received very little recompense for the cases I have conducted for your grandfather. For some years now, I have acted for him in the knowledge that one day . . .'

Jocelyn could no longer stand the sight of his face or the sound of his voice. She passed a bandaged hand across her forehead and clutched at the back of a chair.

'Excuse me, Mr. Creedy,' she said weakly. 'As I told you, I had a fall . . .'

Handing her awkwardly to a chair he asked, "Shall I ring for your maid?"

'If you please. I am sure you will understand it is impossible for me to invite you to stay for dinner.'

'Naturally. Forgive me if I have tired you. But you

were so insistent . . . You would like me to take my leave now?'

She nodded, shielding her face with her hand. It seemed to her that the contempt she was feeling must show in her eyes. Her grandfather had been only too right in his accusation. Thomas had one end in view, the acquisition of her dowry. To that end, he would go to any lengths, within the law, to please Nathaniel Harmer. As for pleasing her, his future wife, he did not, apparently, give a single thought.

When Polly appeared, Jocelyn ordered her to fetch Thomas's hat and whip and show him out. She felt as if all strength had been drained from her. She did not want to move a single muscle, nor even to think. What she desired above all else was to feel Adam's arms about her and to hear him say, as he had done on the ridge of the landslip, 'I am here with you. You are no longer alone.'

What she did hear was Polly's anxious voice. 'Why, ma'am, you look that pale! Won't you let me help you up to your room, and lie down for a space? I'll make it all right with the master, I promise you.'

'Very well,' Jocelyn agreed wearily. 'In truth, I think I *must* rest a while before I face Grandfather and the demands he makes upon me.'

Like a bent old woman, she went slowly up the stairs and along the passage to her bedroom. She lay down fully dressed, and, by the time Polly returned with a hot brick for her feet, she was already half asleep.

Nathaniel ordered peremptorily, 'Open the shutters. I am tired of being in half-darkness. And give me some air.'

Thankfully, Jocelyn pushed back the shutters and opened the casement. An hour ago, while she was having her supper, there had been a short but heavy shower.

The air smelt fresh, and the scent of the wet earth came up to her as she leaned out.

Her grandfather's voice cut across her moment of pleasure. 'Get me out of bed!'

She turned in surprise. 'Do you think that wise? Doctor Marsh did not say . . .'

'I'm not a child, to be told what to do by that drunken quack. Get me out of bed, I say. I want to see what's going on across the valley. I want to see what that fellow Peverell is up to.'

Jocelyn helped the old man to a chair beside the window, and draped a shawl around him.

He asked sharply, 'What have you done to your hands?'

Hastily she put them behind her back. 'I—had a fall.'

'A *fall*? At your age! What were you doing, running helter-skelter down the hill? You always were a hoyden.' He stopped abruptly and glared out of the window. 'Listen to 'em. Bang! Bang! Bang! They never stop. Damned Cavaliers!'

Although Jocelyn could see there were workmen at Galliards, there was not a sound coming from across the valley. There were the usual farm noises from up the lane. The garden-boy was whistling as he hoed the vegetable patch.

Nathaniel's hands gripped the arms of his chair. They looked surprisingly strong. 'Isn't it time I had my medicine?'

'You had it half an hour ago.'

'Bring me a foot warmer. And shut that window, there's a draught.'

Reluctantly, Jocelyn closed the casement and pulled the bell-rope to summon Polly. When the maid had brought the foot-warmer, Nathaniel continued to glare out of the window.

'Where were you all morning?' he demanded.

'At Martha's,' Jocelyn answered guardedly.

'What were you doing all that time?'

She had already prepared her answer for such a question. 'When I fell, I tore my gown. Martha stitched it for me.'

He raised an admonishing finger. 'Don't think you'll get a new one. If you choose to be so careless . . .'

Jocelyn turned away to straighten the bedclothes. 'You need not worry, Grandfather. I know perfectly well that I must keep within my dress allowance.'

He grunted. 'You don't pay for dressing, never did. Not like . . .'

Jocelyn glanced across at him. He was sitting hunched up in the chair, the shawl pulled around his shoulders, his tasselled nightcap a little askew. Despite everything that had happened, she felt a sudden stir of pity. All the affection of which he had been capable had been given to Rosamund, and Rosamund had left him, without a word, for a strolling player she could not have met more than half a dozen times.

He said testily, 'Don't keep fussing about. Come over here!'

When she stood before him, he did not speak for several minutes. Then he asked unexpectedly, 'Where are these children?'

Taken aback, Jocelyn did not reply at once. He repeated the question, glowering up at her.

'They are—not far away,' she answered cautiously. 'Rosamund had been living in Plymouth.'

'In Plymouth? So near, and yet she never came . . . who is looking after them? *His* family?'

'I have never heard anything about her husband's family. They are being cared for by—by someone who hopes to avoid their being sent to the poorhouse.'

He jerked upright as if he had been stung. 'The poorhouse! My great-grandchildren sent to the poorhouse! How dare you!'

It was on the tip of Jocelyn's tongue to say that only the previous evening he had declared they should have been drowned, like kittens.

Instead, she attempted an explanation. 'Rosamund's husband died some months ago, of the smallpox. She herself caught the disease, but recovered. Then she developed a lung infection. I think it likely she did not have sufficient nourishment, for she was evidently almost destitute by then.'

'You knew this, and did not tell me?'

Again, Jocelyn kept her patience. 'No, I did not know, Grandfather. I have had only two letters; one a year after her marriage, the second last week, when she was already dying. Even then, she gave me no address. I was going to tell you of the letters and about the children. But you were taken ill, and Doctor Marsh warned me that you were not to be worried or upset.'

'How dare that drunken quack say what I should or should not be told! What ages are these children?'

'The boy is nine. He has taken on responsibility beyond his years. and even done odd jobs to earn some money, for food. There are two little girls, the youngest under a year. Isabella is four.' Jocelyn paused; then, her heart beating fast, took a risk. 'She is so like her mother that you could believe it was Rosamund herself.'

For a few moments he remained silent, sitting slouched forward again, his chin on his chest. Then he raised his head and his eyes were as fierce as ever.

'Am I to understand you have seen this child?'

Again, she took a risk. 'Yes, I have seen her.'

'And how would you know what Rosamund looked like at four years old? You were not even born then.'

'Martha . . .' She bit her lip, realising her mistake. 'Isabella has big blue eyes and fair ringlets,' she went on hastily, 'and the same mouth. I still remember what Rosamund looked like at seventeen. Besides, there is—

there was, the portrait. One could see from that what she was like as a small child.'

To her intense relief, he seemed satisfied with her explanation. 'Do any of them take after the father?'

'I never saw him, neither in Exeter nor afterwards. The baby, I think, resembles Mama. The boy is very like me.'

He remarked sarcastically, 'Then he deserves some sympathy. You're too tall for a woman and your mouth is too wide, and grey eyes have no character.'

She was too used to his criticism for it to have much effect on her. Besides, in her memory were the words Adam had spoken, 'Even with furze in your hair and chalk dust on your nose, you're still a very beautiful woman.'

Suddenly Nathaniel slumped forward. He would have fallen if Jocelyn had not been quick enough to support him.

'Get me back to bed,' he muttered. 'You've tired me out with all your chattering. You'll be the death of me, you and that obstinate fellow, Creedy. You want me dead, don't you, Jocelyn?'

'No,' she said decisively. 'That I certainly do not.'

For, despite his demands on her, she had some freedom, whereas once married to Thomas Creedy and living in Honiton, she foresaw that she would be tied hand and foot, with even less chance of caring for Rosamund's children.

Nathaniel stood, swaying a little, supported by her arm. She gasped at the pain in her back as she took his weight, but he did not notice. Like Thomas, his concern was entirely for himself.

'You're lying,' he said harshly. 'You never cared a fig for me, not like my little Rosamund. Not like Rosamund, my pretty girl.'

When Jocelyn had helped him back to bed, he lay against the pillows, exhausted. She suggested sending for

Doctor Marsh. But the old man would have none of it.

'Leave me,' he ordered her in a whining tone. 'Leave me alone. I've had a tiring day. That fellow Creedy did me no good, setting himself against me. But I'll show him. I'll show him!' He glared at her from beneath his shaggy eyebrows. 'Why don't you obey me? I told you to leave me alone.'

'Very well, if that is what you wish,' she said resignedly.

She went in search of Polly and instructed the maid to look into the invalid's room from time to time. She attended to one or two tasks, made out a shopping list for when the carrier should next call, then went into the garden to gather some flowers for the house. But her back was aching abominably, and the bandages made it difficult to use her hands. Despite her rest earlier in the day, she felt unutterably weary and very stiff. Since, apparently, her grandfather had no more need of her that day, she decided to go early to bed.

Thankfully, she stretched out on the soft feather mattress. She was dozing when there came a sharp knock on her door. Polly was at her bedside before Jocelyn had roused sufficiently to answer.

'The master's asking for you, ma'am. You'm to come at once, he says.'

Jocelyn sat up too quickly. The room started to spin. Polly caught hold of her arm.

'I'm sorry, I didn't mean to startle you so. 'Tisn't that the master's dying or anything. In fact he's . . .'

The old man's voice sounded along the passage, loud and insistent. '*Jocelyn.* Jocelyn, come here at once. I want you!'

She still felt giddy, and was glad of Polly's support as she put on her white muslin dressing-wrapper. But when she reached Nathaniel's bedroom, she straightened up and went in alone.

He was sitting upright against his propped pillows.

He had regained some colour and his eyes were bright and piercing. One hand was clenched around some object he held against his chest.

'I know you've been lying to me,' he said fiercely. 'But I'm not wasting my strength in getting at the truth. Wherever those children are, go and fetch them.' As Jocelyn gazed at him in utter astonishment, he unclenched his fingers and threw a small purse on to the quilt. 'There's money enough in that for any journey you have to take. Go tomorrow, by whatever means you like.'

Jocelyn sank on to the chair beside the bed. She wondered if she was dreaming. Was it possible that the old man could have changed his mind so completely? Had he, despite every indication to the contrary, some spark of humanity in him?

He soon disillusioned her.

'What's the matter? You look like a puppet with a broken string. Given you a shock, I suppose? Not half as much of a shock as that stubborn lawyer will get when I change my will in favour of my great-grandchildren. That will teach him to argue with me.'

Jocelyn's heart sank. For it was only too plain that his motive in sending for the children was one of spite, not compassion. In that case, would it be wise for them to come? Supposing he should change his mind again and send them away?

If he should threaten that, then she would tell him that she also would leave, and throw herself and the children upon the mercy of Adam Peverell. Such a suggestion was likely to send him into such a rage it might well kill him. But it was the only hold she was ever likely to have over him, and she would use it if ever the need should arise.

She rose and picked up the purse. 'I will carry out your wishes, sir. The two little girls are young enough to need a nurse. Have I your permission to ask Martha to return for as long as proves necessary?'

He made an impatient gesture. 'Do what you wish. Don't bother me, I'm tired. I've done a lot of thinking today. Thought up a fine scheme, but that stubborn fool of a lawyer . . . What are you waiting for? Get back to your room. I don't want you here, looking like a ghost.' He started muttering to himself as Jocelyn made for the door. 'No ghosts here. One in Hawkwood, though. Sir John Peverell's ghost. Saw it once, long time ago. Had a sword in his hand and red hair as long as a woman's. Always were fops, the damned Cavaliers.'

Jocelyn woke late next morning. When, in answer to her summons, Polly came with hot chocolate, she learned it was an hour beyond her usual time of rising.

'I looked in on you once,' the freckle-faced maid told her. 'But you were sound asleep, and so was the master. Are you feeling better this morning, ma'am?'

'I am very stiff, but my hands are not hurting so much. I shall need you to put some more salve on them and bandage them for me, and then help me dress. I have a great deal to do.'

She was about to tell Polly about the children and the need to prepare the nurseries, when the maid said, 'I hope you'll not need to go out, ma'am. There's a sea fret right up the valley, proper thick one, though I dare say 'twill clear later.'

One glance out of the window confirmed Polly's words. It occurred to Jocelyn that a mist would serve her purpose very well, for she might be able to bring the children up from the cottage without their being seen, and then no one could report to her grandfather from which direction they had come. In that case, the sooner she went to fetch them the better. Martha could follow later in the day. As the maid helped her to dress, Jocelyn told Polly briefly about Rosamund's death and that her three children were to be cared for at Penn Barton. The maid stared at her, open-mouthed.

'The portrait, ma'am,' she said, in awe. ' 'Twas her portrait that fell, wasn't it? I told you, 'twould mean a death, didn't I?'

'Yes, indeed,' Jocelyn said impatiently. 'Now listen, Polly. If Grandfather asks for me, tell him I have gone to carry out the instructions he gave me last night. Do not mention the children if you can help it, in case he changes his mind. Once they are here, it will be much more difficult for him to do so.'

The maid nodded her head vigorously. 'I understand, ma'am.' She beamed at Jocelyn. 'It'll liven the place up, won't it, having little ones around? And don't you worry ma'am, I'll help you to keep them out of the master's way.'

Jocelyn smiled at her gratefully. 'You are a good girl, Polly. Tell cook I will see her when I return. And you had better keep silent about the children.'

'Yes, ma'am, that I will. I doubt she'll like the idea of your old nurse coming back. She likes her own way, does cook, and she's a rare one for getting the vapours if she don't have it.'

Jocelyn went quietly from her room and tiptoed along the passage to the landing, and down the stairs. She let herself out of the side door which gave on to the lane.

The mist was thick as she made her way through the village. The street was deserted save for a couple of dogs nosing around the garbage, and a sow with a litter of squealing piglets at her heels. The bleating of the sheep on the high slopes was muffled, and the occasional shout of a farm labourer came eerily through the greyness. When she left the last of the cottages behind, Jocelyn was glad of the chatter of the stream, to guide her down to the beach.

She pulled her cloak more closely about her. The mist, swirling in from the sea, was cold and damp. The cliff path showed only a few feet ahead of her, and she realised that she would have to keep tight hold of the children on her return. As she climbed the stile, she heard the bleating of Martha's goats. It was a pitiable sound, as if they were in some distress. Jocelyn went on up the path, more slowly now. The damp had increased the ache in her back where it had been jarred by her fall, and every step was painful. But her spirits were higher than at any time since she had received Rosamund's letter. The children were to take their rightful place at Penn Barton Manor and she no longer had any need to hide them away and risk Martha being turned out of her cottage. Whatever happened to them now would depend on her. Fortified by a night's sound sleep, her resolve was strong.

Opening the wicket gate, she was again struck by the bleating of the goats. She went around the side of the cottage to the patch of rough ground where they were tethered. To her surprise, she saw that they had not been milked. Another unfamiliar sound reached her ears, the squawking of hens complaining at still being shut up in their house long after they were normally let out.

Jocelyn went quickly back to the cottage and pushed open the door. The little room was empty. There was no answer to her call. She looked into the tiny bedroom, glanced into the wash-house. Puzzled, she went outside and called again. Her only answer was the cry of a seagull, a disembodied sound, coming out of the mist.

Where could Martha be? And why were the hens not let out and the goats unmilked? Jocelyn's heart began to pound as she remembered how Isabella had run away yesterday. In the mist, the cliff was ten times as dangerous. But even if the child had run off, that would not account for the disappearance of Martha, Paul *and* the baby. There must be a simple, reasonable explanation.

When she went back into the cottage, Jocelyn noticed several things she had overlooked before. The fire in the range had almost burned out. Martha's bed had been stripped. Adam's sea-chest was nowhere in sight, nor the little straw mattress Martha had fashioned for Paul.

Jocelyn stood in the deserted cottage, hearing only the ticking of the clock on the mantelpiece. What *could* have happened? Had Martha taken the children away? If so, why? And where? The only danger which threatened them was from their great-grandfather, and he had now relented. There was no sign of fire, or any other disturbance to make Martha quit her home.

At the creak of the gate, Jocelyn rushed to the door. Vaguely, through the mist, she made out the figure of a man, coming up the path. She exclaimed in relief, for it must surely be Adam.

But as the man came nearer, she saw she was mistaken. He was a stranger to her, a short, thickset man dressed in a plain brown suit. His black tricorne was pulled well down over his eyes. He was armed with two pistols and a cutlass.

Jocelyn gasped, then stepped quickly back into the cottage and bolted the door. She glanced around for a weapon. The poker was nearest to hand. She winced as she grasped it too hard. She stood behind the kitchen table, facing the door. She had no means of escape, unless she could scramble through the tiny window in the wash-house.

But there was no time. There came a sharp rap on the door. A man's voice, with a dialect not of Devon, ordered loudly, 'Open up. I am an officer of His Majesty's Customs and Excise. Open up, in the name of the law.'

5

Jocelyn lowered the poker. 'What do you want?' she called.

'I'll tell you that when you've opened the door. Come along now, or 'twill be the worse for you.'

Jocelyn eased the heavy bolt, then stepped back hastily as the door was pushed open. The man came into the room, holding a cocked pistol. He was dark, with blunt features, and strong shoulders and hands. He looked searchingly at Jocelyn, then his gaze went swiftly around the room.

'Sit down,' he ordered peremptorily, 'and tell me what you're doing here.'

Jocelyn drew herself up. 'I think the position is reversed,' she said coldly. 'I am Miss Jocelyn Harmer of Penn Barton Manor. My grandfather's name must be well known to you.'

His manner changed at once. He laid down the pistol and took off his hat.

'Your pardon, ma'am. But I would still ask, with due respect, what your business is here.'

'I cannot think it is of the slightest importance to you, but I came to visit my former nurse.'

'Martha Batten?'

'Yes. But she is not here. In fact, I was . . .'

'About to look for her? That would be useless, ma'am. Martha Batten, along with five fishermen, was taken into custody early this morning on charges of being concerned with smuggling. She is now in Honiton gaol.'

'*What?*' Jocelyn stared at him in dismay. 'You must be

mad! Martha has never been involved in smuggling.'

'May I ask, respectfully, Miss Harmer, how you are so sure?'

'Of course I am sure,' she declared impatiently. 'I have known Martha all my life. Besides, she lives in this cottage by permission of my grandfather, who owns it. You do not suppose she would be so foolish . . .' She broke off abruptly, suddenly realising the full implication of his words.

'You say she was taken away early this morning?'

'That's right.'

'Then . . . Was she alone here?'

He shook his head. 'There were three children in the cottage. There seemed a bit of a mystery about them, some relative's children, she said.'

Jocelyn leaned across the table. 'What happened to them?'

The man shrugged. 'Seeing they're not here now, someone's come for them, I suppose.'

'You mean that you left them here, alone?'

His tone became a little insolent. 'Why not? My duty is to pursue the law, not act as nursemaid to children. The old woman wanted me to take a message, but I'm not a lackey. I'm a Government officer. Besides, she should have thought of them when she broke the law.'

'I am quite sure she has not broken the law,' Jocelyn protested angrily. 'But that must wait. My concern at the moment is for these children. What did you do with them?'

The man frowned. 'I've told you, ma'am, I didn't do anything with them. I left them here. The old woman told the boy someone would come for them.'

'So you left them here? Three small children, alone in a cottage, near to the cliff and in a thick mist?' She thumped the table, wincing at the pain in her hand. 'You had better come and help me search for them.'

She pushed past him, making for the door. Then she remembered the disappearance of Martha's bedding and the sea-chest.

'Did you remove any articles from this cottage?' she demanded of the Preventive Officer.

His tone was truculent. 'Naturally. You don't suppose that, having discovered contraband, I'm going to leave it behind?'

'*Contraband!* But you couldn't have found . . .'

'I'll tell you what I found, Miss Harmer. First, there was some tea . . .'

'You fool! *I* bring tea down to Martha. I suppose you will tell me next that mattresses and bedding are contraband?'

'Not unless they've articles hidden in them, and I found none.'

'Then you did not take these things?' she asked sharply.

He shook his head. 'What I did take was some French lace and silk handkerchiefs.'

She stared at him, realising suddenly what had happened.

'Let me think,' she said, and began pacing up and down the little room.

Could Paul have taken his sisters away from the cottage, hoping to find somewhere to hide, and become lost in the mist? But that would not account for the disappearance of the bedding and sea-chest. The chest was far too heavy for him to carry. Thinking of the sea-chest reminded her of Adam. Could *that* be the answer? Could he have come early to the cottage, learned from Paul what happened, and taken the children to Galliards? In that case, why had he not left her a message? But, of course, he could not do so. There were no writing materials at the cottage.

She must be right, she told herself. Adam *must* have the children. She dared not face any other possibility.

But there was only one way to find out.

'You are quite wrong about Martha,' she snapped at the Preventive Officer as she made for the door. 'Everything can be explained, but I have no time now.'

She ran out of the cottage and down the path. Beyond the gate, the mist was like a damp grey wall, shutting out the valley, the hills opposite, and the sea. She groped her way down the path, chafing at the necessity for going so slowly. Because of the mist, she could not reach Galliards by the quickest route, for she dared not risk the eastern cliff with its criss-crossing of sheep tracks which might lead her toward the cliff edge unawares.

When she reached the combe bottom, she made her way beside the stream for a few hundred yards, then branched off to the right along the course of a small tributary whose source was just below the southern boundary of Adam's land. Trusting to her memory, for she had often come this way in childhood, she believed she would find a path through a copse which would lead her eventually to the back of the house.

She tried not to think of Martha's plight, for she could do nothing for the old nurse at present. She tried to push from her mind any doubts regarding the children's whereabouts. They *must* be at Galliards, she repeated to herself as she scrambled along the bank of the stream, impatiently dragging her cloak free of brambles and gorse. Adam had come for them, she assured herself. He had come, as he always came, when most needed.

The route she had chosen seemed twice as long as she remembered. As she climbed up from the combe bottom, the mist cleared a little and she could see further ahead. But when she came to the copse there seemed no way through it. She went around the edge, and at last discovered the stile she had been looking for, so overgrown it was half-hidden. She tore her cloak as she scrambled over. The path had obviously not been used for years. It was knee-high with rank grass. Fallen leaves made it slippery. Drops of moisture pattered down from the trees. Pigeons, startled by her approach, flew off with a sharp clatter of wings. Some small creature scuttled from beneath her feet, making her start back. With dismay she realised that if she was wrong in her assumption and Paul had taken the children into hiding, they might even now be lost in such a place as this.

The trees thinned. She could see the stile at the end of the path. She clambered over and turned to her right, following the edge of the copse. Momentarily, through a gap in the mist, she saw the outbuildings of Galliards. She ran towards them, stumbling over tussocks of coarse grass in the neglected meadow. Scrambling up a bank, she found herself beside a tumbledown barn, half hidden by briars and elder bushes.

Voices reached her out of the mist. She heard hammering, the sound of a saw biting into wood. She kept to the back of the buildings, not wanting to be seen if she could help it, and reached the corner of the stable.

While she hesitated, trying to decide whether to call Adam's name, she heard footsteps on the gravel. Through a thinner patch of mist she saw, to her joy, his tall figure coming towards her. She ran forward and clutched at his arm.

'Have you got the children?'

'But of course,' he said at once. 'Why are you so distressed? Did you not get my message? I sent a boy . . .'

'Are they all right?' she demanded, breaking into his explanation.

'Perfectly.'

'But where are they? Where have you taken them?'

Adam gripped her elbows. 'Calm yourself. They are here, in the house. The baby is asleep. Isabella is being as good as gold since I promised to continue the story of the pony who escaped from its stable. Paul, as usual, is keeping an eye on both of them. There is not the least need for you to be so anxious. I sent a boy to tell you so. I worded the message so that only you would understand.'

'I must have left before he reached Penn Barton. I set out early because . . .' She realised that if she had not been so eager to take the children home under cover of the mist, she would have been spared the anxiety of the last hour. It had all been unnecessary: the fear, the confrontation with the Preventive Officer, the painful climb up the combe with dread in her heart. She felt suddenly weak, as if her legs would not support her, and near to tears.

Adam's eyes filled with concern. 'Did you go to the cottage?'

'Yes,' she said, and her voice trembled. 'When I found no one there, I was so afraid.'

'It is no wonder you are distressed,' he said sympathetically. 'I am only sorry my message did not reach you in time. I thought it best to bring the children here, for it seemed there was no other place where they could be safe.' He laughed. 'You should have seen us, with a mattress and bedding slung over my horse's back and Isabella demanding to be perched on top of it. Had anyone seen us, they could have taken us for a family of travelling tinkers.'

Footsteps sounded on the gravel. Adam put a hand beneath her arm. 'Let us go into the stable. We shall not be disturbed there.'

When he had led her into the dim building, he pulled an armful of hay from a rack and spread it over some sacking on the floor.

'You will find that tolerably soft and clean, I think.'

'I must not stay,' she protested, although she felt so tired that the thought of taking the children back to Penn Barton dismayed her.

Adam gave an exaggerated sigh. 'Must you insist on running away every time we meet? It is not at all flattering.'

'It is important that I get the children . . .'

'A few minutes cannot make any difference to whatever plan you have in mind. What is important is that you should rest. You are almost spent, and no wonder. You must still be suffering the effects of your fall yesterday.'

As she was about to argue, he laid a finger over her lips. 'No, Jocelyn, I will not listen to you. I insist on your resting for at least ten minutes.'

She sat down on the pile of hay, with Adam beside her, and leaned against the wall. Her back ached abominably. Every muscle seemed stretched to its limit.

Adam took her bandaged hand in his. 'Now sit quietly while I tell you what happened.'

But she was still too tensed up to relax completely.

'I know that Martha has been taken into custody,' she told him. 'The Preventive Officer came while I was at the cottage. He frightened me. He could have been a pirate, he was so heavily armed.'

'He came back?' Adam queried. 'I wonder what for. But that is not our concern.'

'You had heard about Martha? Is that why you went to the cottage?'

He shook his head. 'My intention was to go over every day, to take a rabbit or a pigeon to help with the meals, or anything else that might be needed. I went early this morning so that I should have the cover of the mist. When I got there, I found the children alone and very upset. From Paul I learned that Martha had been taken away, he could not really understand where or why. It was only later that I heard she is suspected of hiding contraband.'

'It is all a mistake,' Jocelyn declared. 'What the Preventive Officer discovered were some articles belonging to you, which we took out of your sea-chest—French lace and silk handkerchiefs.'

Adam slapped his leg. 'What a fool I was to leave them there! But it never occurred to me that anyone could suppose Martha to be involved with smuggling. I assure you I paid full customs on those things. They were bought as presents for my sisters.'

'Poor Martha,' Jocelyn said regretfully. 'She must have thought it necessary to keep silent about them for my sake, and the children's.'

Gently Adam pressed her hand. 'Do not worry your head about her any more. I will ride into Honiton as soon as possible and settle the matter. I imagine that I can do it easily enough without revealing my association with you or Martha, which might lead to the whole story coming out. You would not want that?'

'Indeed, no. Especially now, when Grandfather . . . But how can you get Martha freed, if you do not tell the magistrate that the articles belonged to you?'

He shrugged nonchalantly. 'It will simply mean paying a fine, and perhaps a word in the magistrate's ear that the Preventive Officer was over-zealous.'

'You make it sound so simple,' she said, a little enviously.

He smiled at her. 'Life is full of mountains. I see no point in wasting time and energy on dealing with mole-hills. Our present mountain would seem to be—what to do with these children.'

'Oh, that is all settled. I have had no time yet to tell you.'

When she related the happenings of the previous night and her grandfather's change of heart, she saw growing incredulity on Adam's face. He was silent for a few minutes after she had done, frowning down at his boots.

Then he asked, 'Do you think it wise to take the children to Penn Barton? You are accepting a heavy responsibility. You told me you are not used to children, though you are learning fast and Paul is already devoted to you. But will they be happy there? Supposing your grandfather turns against them again? Will *you* be able to protect them? Are you not attempting something beyond even your strength of purpose?'

'What else would you suggest?' she asked, a little piqued by his doubt of her ability. 'Besides, Grandfather has given permission for Martha to come back. It all seemed to be going so smoothly, and then . . .'

'The children could stay here,' he said. 'Conditions at present are a little uncomfortable, but when the house is finished . . .'

Jocelyn withdrew her hand from his clasp. 'It is very kind of you, Captain Peverell. But I could not think of it. These children are my responsibility. Besides, for the children of a Harmer to be cared for by . . .' She broke off at the sudden realisation of what his offer could mean.

She said excitedly, 'If Grandfather should change his mind, and threaten to send them away, I could tell him that they would always find a home at Galliards. Nothing in the world would induce him to allow that. Which means, they are safe.' She turned to him impulsively. 'I am sorry if I sounded ungrateful, Captain Peverell. Indeed, there seems no limit to your kindness.'

'My name is Adam,' he reminded her. 'The feud between our families may be useful to you for the sake of the children. But it is for us to end it, once and for all.'

'It will never be ended as long as my grandfather is alive,' she said sadly. 'As it is, he is planning some means of harming you.'

'*Harming* me? How the devil does he think to do that? An old man of eighty?' He laughed derisively. 'After surviving almost twenty years at sea I am scarcely likely to shiver in my shoes at your grandfather's threats.'

'You should not underrate him,' she warned him

gravely. 'Because he is confined to his bedroom at present does not mean that he is not without power to harm you. There is a lawyer . . .'

'A *lawyer?*' Adam repeated contemptuously. 'What does that signify?'

'He will ferret out any possible . . .'

'Misdeeds?' Again Adam laughed at the idea. 'You may rest assured he will not succeed in getting me into court. I have my faults, like all men, but they are not such as would land me in gaol or on the gallows. I am touched by your warning, Jocelyn. But I pray you, do not add concern for me to your anxieties. I am perfectly able to take care of myself.'

He sprang lightly to his feet and held out his hand. 'Now that you are rested, I will accompany you and the children to Penn Barton. You need not look so alarmed. Should we meet anyone on the way I promise to melt away like Sir John Peverell's ghost.'

As they left the stable he declared cheerfully, 'I'faith, I have not done so much skulking since I was a boy playing at American settlers and Red Indians.'

Paul, about to mount the steps to Penn Barton, looked up. 'Is this where we're to live, Aunt Jocelyn?'

'Yes. This was your mother's home. She was born here.'

'Will we *stay* here? I mean, we won't have to run away and hide again?'

'No, not any more,' she answered, determined that Paul should not share any doubts she might have.

'Where is the horse?' Isabella demanded. 'I want to see the horse.'

'Not now,' Jocelyn said, freeing her hair from the baby's grasp. 'Later, you can see my pony.'

'I want to see it *now.*'

Jocelyn was about to argue, when she had an inspiration. 'It has gone out for the day, on an adventure, just like the pony Captain Peverell told you about.'

The little girl eyed her suspiciously. 'When will it be back?'

'Tonight, I expect. We will go and see it tomorrow, and if you are good you may have a ride.'

Isabella gave an exaggerated sigh. 'Why do I have to be good? Papa didn't mind me being naughty. He used to laugh.'

Jocelyn shepherded them up the path to the house. Polly had seen them coming, and had the door open.

'Let me take the baby from you, ma'am.' She tickled Sarah under the chin. 'There's a pretty girl.'

Isabella planted herself in front of the maid. '*I'm* the pretty girl. That's what Papa called me.'

Polly laughed. The little girl stamped her foot.

'You're not to laugh at me. I don't like it.'

Jocelyn, exasperated by the difficult time the child had given her on their way to Penn Barton, said sharply, 'You will have to get used to a deal of things you don't like, Isabella. You will not get all your own way with me, I can assure you.'

Isabella pouted. 'Then I want Papa to come back . . .'

'Don't be silly,' Paul said, echoing Jocelyn's impatience. 'You know he can't come back. He's dead.'

Isabella immediately started wailing, though Jocelyn could see no tears.

'Take them up to the day nursery,' she told Polly. 'I must go and talk to cook.'

The maid was about to carry out Jocelyn's instructions when she paused. 'I forgot to tell you, ma'am, Doctor Marsh is here.'

'With Grandfather?'

Upstairs, a door opened and shut. Jocelyn recognised the doctor's heavy tread along the passage. He stopped on the first landing and stared in astonishment at the little group.

'Damme, 'tis true, then!' he exclaimed, coming slowly down the stairs. 'The old scoundrel was babbling on about his great-grandchildren coming here, and how he'd see his pretty Rosamund's girl. I didn't believe a word of it. I thought he'd completely lost his wits.'

'It is quite true,' said Jocelyn, motioning to Polly to take the children upstairs. 'It is Grandfather's wish that they should be given a home here.'

The doctor stared after the two little girls, then stretched out his arm to bar Paul's way. He looked searchingly at the boy, then at Jocelyn.

'Your *sister's* boy?' he asked and there was an insolent note in his voice.

'Certainly,' Jocelyn answered coldly. 'Let him pass, if you please.'

Doctor Marsh stared after him, rubbing his chin. Then he turned to Jocelyn, with a chuckle.

'If I hadn't known you these ten years, I would have sworn . . .'

'I am quite aware that Paul resembles me very closely. But, since you *have* known me for that length of time, Doctor Marsh, there is no need to pursue the subject.'

The doctor pulled a face. 'Odd's faith, now I've offended you. You're a damned touchy woman, Miss Harmer. I suppose if I enquire what hurt you have done to your hands, you'll snap my head off.'

'They were injured in a fall I had yesterday.'

'Should I not examine them?'

'There is no need. Polly has put salve on them and my skin heals quickly. Tell me, Doctor Marsh, what effect do you think the children's presence will have upon Grandfather's health?'

He came heavily down the last few stairs. 'I'd say they'll have one of two effects. Either they'll put new life into him or else . . .'

'Or else?' Jocelyn prompted as he paused.

'They'll drive him into such a rage that he'll burst a blood vessel and so kill himself.' He looked at her consideringly. 'I wonder which you would prefer. After all, if the old scoundrel takes to the children, he may well cut you out of his will.'

'These children are orphans. It is my earnest desire that they may find a home here and that my grandfather will consider it his duty to make provision for their future.'

'Ah, yes!' the doctor exclaimed sarcastically. 'Pious as always, Miss Harmer.'

She turned away, thankful that he could not see into her mind. She would rather bear his jibes than that he should know the thought that had suddenly occurred to her. If his words should come true, and her grandfather change his will in favour of one or all of the children, that might well rob her of any dowry. Without a dowry, she would hold no attraction for Thomas Creedy. If he knew her to be without a penny of her own he would surely be only too willing to rescind the contract of marriage between them.

The tapping of a stick on the floor above brought her sharply back to the present. She went swiftly up the stairs, taking off her cloak which had now had such hard treatment that it was scarcely fit to wear.

Nathaniel was sitting upright against his pillows, his eyes bright and alert.

'Are they here?' he asked at once. 'Have you fetched my great-grandchildren?'

'Yes, sir,' she said obediently, determined that no word or action of hers should spoil things now. 'At what time do you wish to see them?'

'What *time?* I want to see them now, of course. Bring them here at once.'

'Very well. I will just make sure that they are clean and tidy.'

'Why shouldn't they be?' he demanded. 'Where have

you brought them from, the poorhouse? If so, they'll likely have vermin.'

'No, not from the poorhouse. They have been properly looked after, I assure you. I meant simply, that I would comb Isabella's hair and . . .'

'Don't fuss, Jocelyn. I never met a woman who fussed so. Do as I tell you, without arguing.'

Five minutes later, Jocelyn stood outside the bedroom door, the baby in her arms, a child on either side of her. She glanced down at Isabella. So much depended on the conduct of this spoiled and wayward child, so like her great-grandfather's 'pretty little Rosamund'. It remained to be seen whether Isabella, like her mother before her, could twist him around her little finger.

In answer to the old man's summons, Jocelyn shepherded them into the room. He tapped with his stick on the floor.

'Bring them here so that I can see them properly.'

The little group stood by the side of the bed. There was anxiety on Paul's face, open curiosity on Isabella's. The baby regarded him solemnly, a finger in her mouth.

The old man's dark eyes looked searchingly at each child. When he had done, he leaned back.

'Take the baby away,' he ordered. 'Keep it out of my sight. If I so much as hear a sound of it, I shall order you to give it to one of the village women to care for. D'you understand?'

Seeing that Paul was about to protest, Jocelyn gripped his shoulder warningly.

'Yes, sir, I understand,' she said meekly. 'I will make sure that you are not even aware there is a baby in the house.'

Nathaniel prodded Paul in the stomach with his stick. 'Now, you. What's your name?'

The boy's answer to this indignity was to give his great-grandfather a little bow.

'My name is Paul, sir, if you please,' he said politely.

'You look too thin, but don't think you're going to stuff yourself at my expense. I'll decide later what's to be done with you. To send you to boarding-school would cost a lot of money.'

'There's no need for that, sir,' Paul said eagerly. 'Captain . . . Oh.' He winced as Jocelyn's fingers dug into his shoulder.

'Wait until your great-grandfather tells you to speak,' she warned him.

Paul hung his head. 'I'm sorry, ma'am.'

'What's he say? What's he say?' Nathaniel demanded. 'Never could abide a boy who mumbled.'

'He says he is sorry he interrupted you.'

'Then he should have said it so that I can hear. He not only looks like you, Jocelyn. He mumbles like you do. Take him away. I don't want him, either. Now . . .'

His eyes softened as he looked at Isabella. The little girl had been standing, unusually still and quiet, her gaze not moving from the old man in his nightshirt and tasselled cap. He beckoned to her.

'Come here, child, come closer. Let me look at you.'

A little doubtfully, Isabella went right up to the bed. Jocelyn held her breath, while Nathaniel studied the child from head to foot. He curled one of her ringlets around his bony finger. Her blue eyes widened, but she did not draw away.

The old man murmured softly, 'Rosamund. My little Rosamund.'

'My name's Isabella, not Rosamund,' the child protested.

Paul glanced anxiously up at Jocelyn. She gave him a brief smile, but her heart was beating fast. In the next few moments, she believed, the fate of all three children would be decided.

'Yes, yes, I know it's Isabella,' Nathaniel said tetchily.

'But I shall call you Rosamund, because you remind me of your Mama, of whom I was very fond.' He turned to Jocelyn. 'Lift her up here.'

Isabella made no protest. She sat cross-legged beside the old man, surveying him with grave interest. Tentatively she stretched out her hand and tweaked the tassell of his nightcap. Jocelyn gasped in dismay. Then, to her amazement, she saw that the old man was smiling. She could not remember the last time she had seen him smile; not like this, with real pleasure. Isabella giggled and repeated the performance. Nathaniel cackled with laughter.

'Clever Rosamund. Clever little girl.'

He glared at Jocelyn. 'What are you standing there for? I told you to take those two away. This is the one I want.'

Jocelyn hesitated. Would her grandfather remain in this mood? Was it safe to leave Isabella with him?

The little girl put her hand into the old man's and turned to Jocelyn. 'You heard what he said,' she declared imperiously. 'Go away.'

Again Nathaniel cackled delightedly. 'That's right, my pretty Rosamund, that's right. Jocelyn, fetch some toys. Dolls, picture-books, ludo—they must all be in the nursery still. Fetch them all down. And open the shutters wide. I begin to feel better. My little Rosamund's come back. That's worth more than all the hateful medicine that damned quack gives me.'

Jocelyn handed the baby over to Polly and went to look for the toys, taking Paul with her. While she rummaged in cupboards, he stood at the window, not saying a word.

When she straightened up, with an armful of toys, he asked her, 'Is that Captain Peverell's house?'

She joined him at the window. The mist had almost cleared now.

'Yes, that is Galliards.'

He was frowning, and his shoulders drooped. 'If I'm not wanted here, Aunt Jocelyn, I could go there. Captain Peverell said . . .'

Jocelyn dropped the toys on the window seat and put an arm about him. 'Paul, dear, you must not mind what Grandfather says. He is a very old man and unwell. He loved your mother very much, and Isabella is so like her. That is why he is making such a fuss of her, and taking little notice of you.' She took his face between her hands. 'You must not even think of going away, Paul. *I* want you here. I have been very lonely and shall be glad of your company. You will be able to help me in so many ways. Will you believe that?'

He regarded her gravely for a moment or two. Then he smiled and nodded.

'Yes, Aunt Jocelyn. I should like to stay with you until Captain Peverell says I can go to sea with him.' He stood up straight and squared his shoulders. 'How can I help you?'

Jocelyn felt an almost overwhelming desire to hug him. But she knew how much he valued his independence, and his aversion to being treated as a girl. She smiled and kissed him lightly on the forehead.

'You can carry down some of these toys. Then we will go to the stable and you may exercise my pony by walking him round the yard.'

He looked pleased. Then his expression changed to one of surprise. 'But you told Isabella that your pony wasn't there.'

She put a hand over her mouth. 'Oh dear, now I *have* given myself away.'

Paul's eyes widened. 'You told a *fib*, Aunt Jocelyn?'

'It was only a very little one, just to keep Isabella quiet.'

His face took on the mischievous expression she had

seen when he pretended to be one of Martha's goats. 'I won't tell. I won't tell anyone.'

'Thank you,' she said gravely. Then, suddenly, she was laughing and Paul was joining in.

As they left the nursery, she heard the unfamiliar sound of laughter coming from her grandfather's bedroom. Jocelyn's spirits rose. If only Isabella could keep the old man enchanted, just as Rosamund had done, the future might be a great deal brighter than had ever seemed possible.

6

'There, my lamb,' Martha said with satisfaction, as she lifted Sarah on to her lap, 'proper bonny you look in your mother's coat and bonnet.' She smiled happily at Jocelyn. 'I never thought to see this nursery again. In fact, this time yesterday I thought 'twas the inside of a gaol I'd be seeing for some time to come. How do you suppose Captain Peverell had me freed so soon, ma'am? He told me there'd been no need to say that 'twas his things the Preventive Officer found in my cottage.'

'He spoke of a fine,' Jocelyn answered, 'and that it could easily be paid. He seems to make light of all difficulties, Martha. But I owe him so great a debt now.'

'I don't reckon he considers it in that light. 'Tis my belief he's the kind of man who always has to be helping folks.' The old woman dandled Sarah on her knee, her forehead creased in thought. 'I do hope Captain Peverell didn't really march straight into the magistrate's house and threaten him with a drawn sword.'

'Is that what he told you he did?' Jocelyn asked in amusement.

'Aye, though I think he was probably joking. To tell the truth, Miss Jocelyn, I'm not at all sure when he's being serious and when he's teasing.'

'Neither was I, at first, but I am beginning to know him better now. I think he would laugh in the midst of the greatest danger. Certainly my spirits rise when I am with him.'

'And your eyes light up every time his name is spoken. He talked a lot to me as he brought me back on his horse from Honiton this morning, and the more he talked the more I thought what a fine man he is, kind and brave and generous. It seems he comes of a very united family. All his sisters are married and his mother's been seeking a wife for him for years. Every time he comes home from the sea she has a dozen or more young ladies lined up for his inspection—just like horses at a sale, he said. But that's not the way he'd want to choose a wife, I'm thinking.' Martha shook her head sadly. 'Oh, my dear, if only you were free.'

Jocelyn stood by the open nursery window, resting her hands on the bars. From this height, the view of Galliards was unimpeded. She could see workmen moving about, small as insects from this distance, and smoke rising from a chimney. She could picture Adam there, directing them with his usual cheerful good nature and ready smile. She shut her eyes, seeing his face in every detail, feeling again the strength of his arms about her, hearing the warmth of his voice.

She sighed as she turned back to Martha. 'But I am not free. Nor as things stand at present, shall I ever be.'

Martha stood up, the baby in her arms. Her tone changed as she said, 'Let's not look too far ahead, Miss Jocelyn. Until the day you're actually standing at the altar beside that dry stick of a lawyer, there's always hope something will prevent the marriage. 'Tis possible Mr. Harmer will have a change of heart now the children are here.'

'The only one who will change *his* heart is Isabella,' Jocelyn said ruefully. 'It is a miracle the difference in him already. He seems to have recovered most of his strength.'

The old nurse sniffed. 'You may call it a miracle, ma'am. I'd say what's happened is natural. They both want their own way above all things, and both have got it. The master wanted Miss Rosamund back and he's pretending to himself that he's got her. Miss Isabella, just like her mother, must always be the centre of attraction, and have someone to spoil her. Old fool that he is, Mr. Harmer . . .' She put a hand to her mouth. 'I shouldn't have said that, ma'am, not now I'm back in service at Penn Barton. Now, I'm going to take this little one out into the sunshine. Where's Master Paul?'

'Helping the garden boy. I know he grieves for Rosamund and must miss her dreadfully. But he is so brave and so anxious to please me. I have grown very fond of him, Martha. I only hope I can keep him out of the way when Grandfather comes downstairs, as he swears he will do within a day or two whatever Doctor Marsh may say.'

'I kept you and Master William out of his way for many years,' her old nurse reminded Jocelyn. 'I'm not so old I can't do the same again, if it means protecting this babe and the boy from the master's temper.'

Jocelyn put an arm about the old woman's shoulder. 'I have said it before, Martha, and I say it again. You are such a blessing to me.'

Martha gave Jocelyn a considering look. 'If that's how you feel, I wonder if you'd do me a kindness.'

'Of course. What is it?'

' 'Tis my goats. They'll not have been milked for nigh on two days, and 'twill go badly with them. And the chickens won't have been let out or fed.'

Jocelyn patted her shoulder. 'That is easily seen to. I will go myself.' She laughed. 'Do you remember when you taught me to milk the goats?'

'I do, indeed. They're difficult creatures, goats, until they get to know you.' She glanced anxiously at Jocelyn. 'When will you go, ma'am. This evening?'

'Should I not go sooner?' Jocelyn asked in surprise.

Martha shook her head. 'No, this evening will do nicely, and I dare say you've tasks to do about the house before then. And I'd be glad if you'd bring back with you one or two things I'll be needing—that is, if that interfering customs man hasn't walked off with all I possess.'

Jocelyn was half-way to the cottage that evening before she realised that it was most unlikely she would be able to do any milking with her bandaged hands. They were healing cleanly but were still painful, especially when she tried to grip anything or put any pressure on her palms. If she found the task impossible, she supposed it would be best to bring the goats up to Penn Barton. She paused beside the stream, wondering if it would not be better to wait until morning, and then take Paul with her to help. Then she remembered the hens needed feeding, and fresh water, and there would be eggs to collect.

Walking through the water meadows, she enjoyed the beauty of the warm spring evening. The hawthorns were in bud; there were primroses and bluebells in the hedgerows, gorse in full bloom on the slopes of the combe. A lark rose from near her and flew, singing rapturously, up into the pale blue sky. Following its flight, Jocelyn saw, high overhead, a buzzard drifting the length of the valley, tipping and tilting its wide, fringed wings to gain the best advantage from the air currents. A shepherd whistled to his dog on the eastern hillside. From further up the valley she could hear the chanting of a ploughman and his boy as they drove their team of oxen.

A sense of peace enveloped Jocelyn. For the moment, her problems seemed at an end. The children were safely at Penn Barton, her grandfather won over by Isabella. Martha, thanks to Adam, had come to no harm. She herself was recovering from the terrifying experience of her fall down the cliff. As to her future, there was nothing she could do but wait.

She recalled Adam's words. 'Life is full of mountains, do not waste time and energy on molehills.'

She would regard her marriage to Thomas Creedy as a molehill, far away in the distance.

Jocelyn was singing to herself as she walked up the cliff path and climbed the stile. She was almost at the wicket gate when she heard a commotion behind the cottage. The goats were bleating loudly and she could hear the thud of their hooves on the ground. By the screeching of the hens, Jocelyn realised they were outside their house. Thinking that a fox was amongst them, she ran round the side of the cottage. Then she stopped abruptly.

Adam, his clothes dishevelled, his hair loose on his shoulders, was sitting on the grass. He was making wild attempts to milk the biggest of the nanny-goats, a determined animal which sometimes stubbornly refused to be milked even by Martha.

As Jocelyn looked on in astonishment, the goat gave a tremendous bound, knocking over the pail. Adam fell backwards. The milk spilled over his breeches. He let out an oath fiercer and more expressive than any her grandfather used.

She could not help herself. She burst out laughing. Adam, attempting to rise, glanced in her direction. While his attention was diverted, the goat butted him heavily in the stomach. He let out a yell and aimed a fist at the animal. The goat, retreating, dragged the tethering rope around Adam's ankles. He fell sprawling. Jocelyn doubled up with laughter. Then, controlling herself, she ran forward.

'Let me help you.' She took hold of the goat's collar and tugged the creature away.

With some difficulty, Adam extricated himself from the rope and stood up, trying with little success to wipe the milk from his breeches.

'I never met such a wayward creature,' he declared. 'I was only trying to help her, she had such a full bag.'

'It was good of you,' Jocelyn said, feeling rather

ashamed of herself. 'I am sorry I laughed, it was unkind.'

He took her gently by the shoulders. 'Don't be sorry, Jocelyn. It is so good to hear you laugh, so good to see you look like this, young and untroubled. This was how you looked the first time I saw you. You were wearing a green and yellow gown, and an absurd straw hat tilted at the most provocative angle . . . You were a sight to gladden the heart of a sailor back from many months at sea as you came down the hillside, singing.'

And she had seen a young man sitting on the stile, and wanted him to kiss her. He had been a stranger, then. He was not a stranger now. And, more than ever, she wanted him to kiss her.

As if he had read her thoughts in her eyes, he drew her towards him. His fingers stroked her hair, caressed the nape of her neck.

'Jocelyn,' he said softly. 'I fell in love with you that very day. I fell in love with a beautiful girl with dark hair and grey eyes who would not tell me her name.' He took her face between his hands. 'I wanted to kiss you. But you were afraid. Are you still afraid, Jocelyn?'

She shook her head. 'I was not afraid then—not of you. I was—startled, that I could feel as I did, that I should want you to . . .' She lowered her eyes, feeling the colour rising to her cheeks. 'It did not seem right, somehow, that I should want you to kiss me.'

'So that was why you drew away? And I thought I had offended you. Look at me, Jocelyn.'

When she did so, he bent his head towards her and kissed her full on the lips. She put her arms about his neck and responded with all the passion she had stifled for so long.

When, at last, they drew apart, Adam declared fiercely, 'I cannot wait for you, my darling! I cannot wait until your grandfather dies for you to be free. I shall call upon him.'

'Oh, no!' Jocelyn exclaimed in dismay. 'Adam, you must not. If you did, it would mean I could not even meet you.'

'Because of this absurd feud between our families? You do not really suppose I shall allow that to keep us apart, surely? I shall kidnap you, elope.'

She shook her head. 'You know that is impossible. I have given my word to stay with Grandfather. He made me swear an oath to remain with him until his death. He was so afraid I would do exactly what you are suggesting, elope like Rosamund.'

'Then what are we to do?' Adam demanded. 'Simply wait patiently for your grandfather to die? I have only until the autumn.'

She jerked up her head. 'What do you mean?'

'I had planned to sail for the East . . .'

'Oh!' The word was a cry of pain.

Adam took her in his arms again. 'So the thought of my going away distresses you? Perhaps I was being cruel, but I was testing you, Jocelyn. I shall not leave you here, to fend for those children against this ogre of a grandfather. I can hire a captain to sail my ship for me, though that will take away some of the profits.'

'You would do that, for me?' she whispered.

'I love you. I want to be near you, always. I want to see you at Galliards, surrounded by our children, to see you happy and laughing, not . . . Why, what is the matter?'

Almost roughly, she freed herself from his arms. She turned away, her hands to her flushed cheeks. What had she done? What madness had seized her, to let Adam make love to her, and to reveal her own feelings to him?

'What is it, my love?' he asked gently. 'What is troubling you? Is it the thought of the children? You know I would take them, too.'

'Please, oh please, Adam, don't say any more.' She buried her face in her hands.

She knew what she must do. She must tell him, swiftly and honestly, that it was useless his waiting, for she would never be free. She must confess to keeping silent about the contract of marriage. Whatever the consequences, it was not fair to keep him any longer in ignorance of the fact that she was betrothed to another man.

She tried to form the words in her mind. Her lips moved soundlessly. Then, quite clearly, she saw what it would mean. The love in Adam's eyes would change to scorn as he realised that she had cheated him. He would turn from her, never want to see her again. And she knew suddenly that was more than she could bear. She had so lately and unexpectedly come to this wonderful happiness. She could not turn her back on it, not yet.

She flung herself into Adam's arms, hiding her face against his chest. He did not question her about her sudden distress. His hands, warm and strong, caressed her. His voice was gentle, reassuring. She clung to him, and fought back the tears of shame which welled into her eyes. She had accepted Adam's help, leaned upon his strength, sought comfort in his presence, and given nothing in return. As far as she could see, she never would. Instead, however long she might delay it, the day would come when she would be forced to hurt him terribly. One day she would have to say to him, 'I have taken all, and now you must go. Despite your promise to me, your devotion, your love, I am not for you, nor ever will be.'

'But not yet,' she cried inwardly. 'I am not strong enough yet.'

On Sunday morning, since her grandfather still kept to his room, Jocelyn took Paul to church. This caused a stir amongst the congregation equal to that occasioned by the occupation, for the first time in over twenty years, of the ornately carved Peverell pew. From across the aisle, all Jocelyn could see of Adam was his cinnamon-coloured stockings and silver buckled shoes, but she was very conscious of his presence, only a few yards from her.

Paul sat very still and upright beside her throughout the long sermon. Jocelyn was used to the ageing parson's faltering words, his habit of straying from the point and engaging a member of the congregation in a conversation which would have been more fittingly conducted in the village street or upon a farm. She was used, too, to the chatter and laughter of the village boys behind her, until they were summarily dealt with by the dog-whipper.

She felt very proud of her nephew. Not once did she have to give him so much as a warning glance, though she heard him sigh occasionally and noticed his gaze stray hopefully to the hour-glass upon the clerk's desk below the high pulpit.

It was the custom of the congregation to wait for Nathaniel Harmer to make his slow way down the aisle before they moved from their seats. Now, at the end of the service, all eyes turned expectantly to the Peverell pew. Without haste, Adam stepped into the aisle, and came face to face with Jocelyn.

For a moment they looked at each other, across the width of the aisle. Then Adam smiled and moved back to allow her precedence. Very conscious of the rustle of surprise that went through the rows of villagers, she took Paul's hand and, head high, walked down the length of the aisle and out into the sunshine of the spring morning. Her heart was beating fast, and her cheeks felt hot. She would have liked to make her escape at once, so that there should be no possibility of the villagers guessing that she and Adam were well acquainted. She was not sure that she could keep up the pretence of not knowing

Adam, or trust Paul to do so. But it would not do to turn her back upon the villagers and make for home without stopping to speak to some of them.

Adam joined her on the cobbled path outside the porch. There were several villagers grouped behind him as he bowed to her. His voice was loud enough to reach them.

'Miss Harmer, I believe, from Penn Barton Manor? I am delighted to make your acquaintance, ma'am. I have heard that your grandfather has been indisposed. I trust he is now making good progress towards recovery.'

Paul giggled, and Jocelyn saw the amusement in Adam's eyes. She answered him in the same formally polite tone he had used, then withdrew a little as the congregation emerged from the church.

One or two women came to speak to her, but all the men immediately surrounded Adam. She noticed that even Henry Blakiston, the foremost of the parish's yeomen farmers, greeted him with marked deference. How furious her grandfather would have been to see this happen. Even the fact that Adam had allowed her to take precedence over him as they left the church, would probably be twisted by the old man so as to increase his animosity.

The doctor's voice sounded at her elbow. 'Our new "lord of the manor" seems to have made himself popular already. But then, if a man has sufficient money to be able to offer bribes . . .'

'Bribes?' Jocelyn repeated.

He looked at her in surprise. 'Have you not heard about it? But you must have done, Miss Harmer, for your own nurse is one of those whose release Captain Peverell secured.'

'One of them? Do you mean that Captain Peverell has . . . ?'

'He has paid the fines of all the men taken on charges

of smuggling. You know what that means? Since none of them would have been able to afford the fines imposed on them, he has saved them from long terms of imprisonment.'

'How very generous!' she exclaimed spontaneously. 'But then, it is so like him.'

She realised her mistake as she saw the glint in the doctor's eyes.

'Am I to suppose from that remark, that you are acquainted with Captain Peverell? Perhaps you have met him on one of those long walks you take for the good of your health.'

She said coldly, 'You have already mentioned that he secured Martha's release. Surely it is evident, therefore, that he is a man of . . .'

'Undoubted generosity? Quixotic impulses?' The doctor rubbed his chin thoughtfully. 'I wonder. I very much wonder. He's a man of the sea, used to handling cargoes, and 'tis said he's been seen more than once on the cliffs, with a telescope.'

'And from such gossip,' she said bitingly, 'are you about to deduce that he has joined the freetraders?'

He looked at her speculatively. 'There are a deal more unlikely things happen in life. And 'twould not be the first time Galliards has been used as a hiding-place. But he'd best take care, our gallant Captain. For I doubt that the new Preventive Officer is a man to be scared off by a ghost of a long-dead Cavalier.'

Jocelyn made an excuse to leave him and spoke a few words to the blacksmith's wife, then made her way to the lych-gate. As she and Paul started up the hill towards Penn Barton, she saw that Adam was still the centre of a group of villagers. The men's deep voices were unusually animated and Jocelyn could hear them laughing. It was fortunate, she thought, that her grandfather was not here. Such evidence of Adam's immediate popularity would have thrown him into one of his uncontrollable rages.

Paul asked, 'Why did you pretend not to know Captain Peverell? I thought it was all right now that Great-grandfather has taken us in.'

'No, Paul, it is far from all right. You must never let Grandfather know that Captain Peverell was so kind to you and your sisters. You must promise me never to mention his name in front of Grandfather.'

'I promise,' the boy said reluctantly. 'But why mustn't I, Aunt Jocelyn?'

'It is a long story. I will tell it to you while we walk home. It started over a hundred years ago, in the time of King Charles . . .'

They had reached the gate of Penn Barton by the time she had finished. She had been so absorbed in making the feud between the families easy for Paul to understand, that she was brought up sharply by the sight of Thomas Creedy's grey cob tethered to the ring in the wall.

She put a hand to her mouth. 'Oh, I had forgotten. Paul, go up to Martha and tell her you will all be having dinner in the nursery.'

'Must I go quietly, and not be seen?' he asked gravely.

She put a hand on his shoulder. 'No, dear, those times are past. It does not matter in the least if Mr. Creedy sees you. He is Grandfather's lawyer and comes to dinner on Sundays.'

'What is a lawyer?' Paul asked.

'I will explain later. I have no time now, for I must make sure that Mr. Creedy has been offered some wine.'

The boy looked up at her. 'Don't you like Mr. Creedy?'

'Whatever made you ask that?' she demanded, startled.

'You don't look happy. You don't look a bit like you do when you meet Captain Peverell.'

She said lightly, 'You see too much for a boy of your age.'

He grinned at her. '*You'd* better not let Isabella see the horse, Aunt Jocelyn. She'll be wanting to ride it if she does.'

Jocelyn said urgently, 'Paul, make sure she is kept away. Mr. Creedy would never allow such a thing.'

The boy sighed. 'Whatever else there is to put up with at sea, there won't be Isabella.'

Jocelyn shook her head at him, laughing. 'You know you are very fond of her, really.'

He pulled a face. 'I suppose so,' he agreed reluctantly. 'But she *is* a trial.'

To Jocelyn, his words were an echo of her own, spoken so many times in years gone past, about Rosamund. It was to be hoped that Isabella would not cause as much unhappiness to her brother as Rosamund had brought upon her own sister.

Jocelyn found Thomas in the drawing-room. As it was Sunday, he was wearing, not his legal black, but the new brown velvet suit with the gold waistcoat. She saw at once that something had displeased him. He scarcely gave her time to sit down before he voiced his grievance.

'Miss Harmer, I do think you might have warned me that there were children at Penn Barton. I cannot abide children of any age, as I should have thought I had made abundantly clear to you.'

Jocelyn, seeing that his glass was already full, poured herself some wine. She said calmly, 'You may rest assured they will be kept out of your way. I have just told my nephew that they will take their dinner in the nursery today. Usually, the two older ones join me in the dining-room.'

'The little girl was certainly not kept out of my way,' Thomas said testily. 'She came running along the path the moment I arrived and demanded—positively *demanded*—to be given a ride on my horse.'

Jocelyn bent her head to hide a smile. The picture of Thomas confronted by Isabella was one which gave her some amusement.

'I am sorry you were caused annoyance,' she apologised. 'Isabella, I fear, is a headstrong child.'

'So I have learned from your nurse,' he said icily. 'She told me that Mr. Harmer dotes on the child.'

'That is true. He was devoted to my sister Rosamund.'

Thomas pursed his thin lips. 'I am surprised to hear you say that. I was under the impression that your sister's name was wholly discredited and never spoken in this house.'

Jocelyn leaned back and sipped her wine. She was beginning to enjoy the situation.

'That has all changed, Mr. Creedy. In fact, as my grandfather may have mentioned to you, he is even talking of changing his will in the children's favour.'

'What?' He gulped his wine too quickly, and spluttered. 'I have not been informed of any such intention. What is more, I have not even been allowed up to Mr. Harmer's room. If he is well enough to endure the company of a small child, then I should have thought . . .'

'I will speak to him, after dinner,' Jocelyn promised, not wanting to lose any opportunity for her grandfather to instruct the lawyer to redraft his will.

Thomas drew himself up. 'I shall be obliged if you will, Miss Jocelyn. Quite apart from the fact that I should advise him that it would be unwise—most unwise—to bequeath his property to minors, even if he should place them under my jurisdiction . . .'

'*Your* jurisdiction? Why should he do that?'

He raised his eyebrows. 'Is it not obvious? When your grandfather dies, you will become my wife. If—mistakenly in my opinion—you are determined to make these children your responsibility, they naturally become mine.'

'Oh, no,' she said firmly. 'If my grandfather does not provide for them, all I ask from you will be to allow me a certain sum for their maintenance. I myself would arrange for them to live, if not here at Penn Barton . . .'

'Penn Barton Manor will be sold,' he reminded her.

'Then at some suitable place where they can be cared for properly, and where I may visit them.'

Very deliberately he placed his glass on the side table. 'I think, ma'am, we should come to an understanding. Naturally, I shall show you every respect and consideration when we are married. But I never allowed either of my wives to have any say whatever in the management of my affairs or in any decisions I may take.'

Jocelyn grasped the arms of her chair. She said angrily, 'My sister's children are not your affair, nor need ever be. Whatever money is spent on them will be from my dowry. Whatever decisions need to be taken, I will take. I promise you I will not try in any way to interfere in your affairs. But I will *not* have those children sent beyond my reach. They have faced too much grief and anxiety already . . .'

'Calm yourself, my dear lady, calm yourself. I really cannot allow you to become so incensed. It is not seemly in a woman. I do assure you, whatever plan I make will be for the best.'

Jocelyn forced herself to relax, to remember Adam's words about the mountain and the molehill. At this stage, the children's future was a molehill which might never develop into a mountain. It was foolish to show such anger in front of Thomas.

'Yes, I am sure it will be,' she said more calmly. 'Will you take some more wine?'

'Thank you, no.' Pompously he pulled out his watch.

'Is it not time dinner was served? Your grandfather is always so prompt.'

She reached out and jerked the bell-rope. It was a few minutes before Polly appeared, looking flustered.

'Cook says to tell you dinner will be ready in ten minutes, ma'am. There's been a little—accident.'

'Accident?' Thomas repeated in alarm. 'What sort of accident? Not to the joint, I trust?'

Polly swallowed hard and looked appealingly at Jocelyn. Seeing her embarrassment, Jocelyn rose.

'If you will excuse me, Mr, Creedy, I will go and find out what has happened. I apologise for keeping you waiting after your long ride.'

'What *has* happened?' she whispered to the maid as they went across the hall to the kitchen.

Polly tittered, then swiftly put up a hand to hide her mirth.

' 'Twas Miss Isabella's fault, really, ma'am. She was teasing cook the way she does, and cook took a wooden spoon to her and . . .' She giggled again. 'Miss Isabella got hold of the toasting fork and chased cook round the table. She managed to prod her, right in the . . .'

Polly could no longer restrain herself. It was some moments before Jocelyn could get any sense out of her.

'Cook was so startled she fell over a stool. Then she had the vapours, and Maisie and me had to burn some feathers under her nose. But she refused to dish up dinner so Maisie and me has had to do it. I do hope 'twill be all right, ma'am. Mr. Creedy is that pernickety.'

'I am well aware of that,' Jocelyn said grimly. 'This may have seemed very funny to you, Polly, but we shall have to bear the consequences if it comes to Grandfather's ears. You may be sure he will not believe that Miss Isabella was responsible. In his eyes, she can do no wrong. Oh well, it cannot be helped.'

Polly, somewhat sobered by Jocelyn's words, asked,

'Will I bring in the dinner now, ma'am?'

'Give me a minute or two to think up some explanation to give Mr. Creedy.'

But as Jocelyn went towards the drawing-room, she changed her mind. Why should she explain to him? She had apologised for the meal being a little later than usual. She owed him no more obligation than that.

During the silent meal, Jocelyn allowed her thoughts to wander. Inevitably they turned towards Adam. How very differently from Thomas had he told her to calm herself. How different was his attitude to her sister's children. But then, how different he was in every way from this middle-aged, cold-natured lawyer who, unless the longed-for miracle happened, would sit across the table from her at every meal in the years to come.

She was jerked out of her reverie by the loud clearing of Thomas's throat.

'I think you have been unaware that I was speaking to you,' he said in a hurt tone.

Hastily she swallowed a piece of rhubarb pie. 'I am sorry. I thought that you disliked talking at mealtimes.'

'Nevertheless,' he said precisely, 'when I do, I expect from you the common courtesy of listening.'

It occurred to Jocelyn that Thomas was showing a new side to his character. Until today, she had not been left alone with him for any length of time. Certainly he would not dare to behave in this high-handed manner in front of her grandfather. He was continuing to speak in the same dictatorial tone.

'I must *insist* on seeing Mr. Harmer. When he knows I have carried out his wishes I am sure he will regret the unjust and uncalled for remarks he made at our last meeting. He will be delighted that we have Captain Peverell just where we want him.'

Jocelyn felt the blood drain from her face. She forced herself to speak calmly.

'You have discovered some facts which are—not in his favour?'

Thomas pushed away his plate. 'I have, indeed. Though they are scarcely what Mr. Harmer had in mind. Unfortunately I could not find any flaw in Captain Peverell's title to Galliards, nor that he had encroached on his neighbours' land. Nor is there any suggestion of his diverting a leat to serve . . .'

'Then what did you find?' Jocelyn broke in, regardless of Thomas's frown of disapproval.

Leaning back, he put the tips of his fingers together. 'Captain Peverell has been indiscreet. He has allied himself to the freetraders—a very dangerous move, especially now that there is at last a really honest and zealous Preventive Officer in the district.'

Recalling the manner in which the doctor had spoken to her about Adam after church, Jocelyn felt a little shiver run down her spine. Yet she felt quite sure that Adam, despite his light-hearted suggestion that he would look for brandy kegs in his barns, was no more involved with smuggling than his openly generous gesture of paying the fines of the arrested men.

'Why should he take to smuggling?' she asked. 'He is a man of considerable wealth, I believe. He would not need . . .'

Thomas's frown did stop her this time. 'If you will allow me to continue, without interruption,' he said severely. 'I did not say Captain Peverell is actively engaged in smuggling. That has yet to be proved. But by setting himself at variance with the law and impeding the proper course of justice, he has inevitably brought upon himself suspicion of having *some* part in freetrading.'

'But surely he has not gone against the law?' she protested. 'Merely by paying fines . . .'

'He offered a sum greater than the fines imposed so

that the men could be released immediately. That, Miss Jocelyn, can be termed bribery.'

'I see.' It was just what Doctor Marsh had said.

Indiscreet though it might be, she could not help rising to Adam's defence. 'Can it not be accepted that he was just being kind? After all, he paid Martha's fine, too, and no one can seriously accuse her of being a freetrader.'

'Martha?' he repeated, looking puzzled.

'The children's nurse whom you met this morning.'

Thomas leaned forward. 'Do you mean to tell me *that* was the woman in whose cottage certain articles of contraband were found?'

'Certainly. Except that it was not contraband.'

'Indeed? Then what were they?'

'They belonged . . .' Realising she had gone too far, she asked, 'Will you take some cheese or fruit?'

But Thomas was not to be put off. 'They belonged, perhaps, to you?'

When she shook her head, he persisted, 'To Captain Peverell, then?'

'Why should they? What would Captain Peverell be doing at Martha's cottage?'

Thomas leaned back, a satisfied expression on his face. 'That, Miss Jocelyn, is just what I am wondering. In fact, it would seem there are more trails to follow than I realised. I do not think my time would be wasted by paying a call upon this gentleman.'

Jocelyn clasped her hands beneath the table. She saw just how foolish she had been in her mistaken attempt to defend Adam. For, even though she was sure no harm could come to him through Thomas Creedy, a meeting between the two men might well lead to her undoing. Although her betrothal to Thomas was known only to Martha, there had been no agreement to keep it secret and there was no real reason why Thomas should not ⌐

speak of it to Adam should the situation call for it. She felt cold at the thought that Adam might learn of it through Thomas before she had had a chance to tell him. Somehow, she must prevent any such possibility.

'You do not appear to be in favour of my plan,' Thomas remarked.

'Would it not be better to leave the matter in the hands of the Preventive Officer? You have already mentioned that he is a zealous man, not likely to overlook any point which might incriminate Captain Peverell. And,' she went on, suddenly inspired, 'should the rumour be true that there is contraband hidden at Galliards, surely a man trained for the task is more likely to find it than you, Mr. Creedy?'

He gave her a long, calculating look out of his pale eyes. To her relief, he appeared to accept her suggestion at face value.

'Perhaps you are right. But, I must confess, your attitude surprises me. I was beginning to suspect, from your previous remarks, that you were acquainted with Captain Peverell and that, for some reason you were not prepared to reveal, were determined to take his part.'

She opened her eyes very wide. 'How could you possibly think that? You must know, as the whole parish knows, that for over a hundred years the Peverells and Harmers have been bitter enemies. Do you really suppose that Grandfather would allow me even to speak to this gentleman? Admittedly, as we came out of church this morning, he greeted me very civilly and naturally I answered him in the same fashion.'

Thomas sat forward. 'And this is the only time you have spoken to him?'

Jocelyn rose from the table. 'Mr. Creedy, I would remind you that we are not yet married. Until we are, I am under no obligation to answer your questions, nor to account to you for my conduct. I will go up to Grandfather now, and enquire whether he will receive you.'

Her heart was beating fast as she went upstairs. Nathaniel was sitting in a chair near the window. There was a tray on the table beside him. He glared at Jocelyn.

'I smelt roast beef. Why wasn't I brought roast beef? You know how partial I am to a good red joint.'

'Doctor Marsh has forbidden you red meat,' she answered patiently.

'Be damned to that drunken quack. Can't he see I'm better? That child has done it. I told you Rosamund was better for me than all his obnoxious medicine.' He gestured violently towards the tray. 'Tell the girl to bring me a proper dinner and take away this baby's pap.'

'Very well, if that is what you wish. I came to tell you Mr. Creedy is still here, asking to see you.'

Nathaniel banged his fist on the arm of his chair. 'I won't see him! I've already said no. Obstinate fellow stood out against me. I told him to find out something that would harm that fellow, Peverell, but he refused.'

Jocelyn remained silent. It was certainly not in her interest to tell him that Thomas had news which he thought would please the old man. From that point of view, she was relieved that her grandfather would not receive Thomas. On the other hand, it would mean that, if he still thought of altering his will, the matter would be further delayed. As things stood at present, she was tied by the marriage contract, and the children not provided for. Since there could be no real danger to Adam, she decided it would be better if Thomas were received.

She said hesitantly, 'You did mention, sir, that you had some idea of changing your will . . .'

The colour mounted ominously into the old man's cheeks. His bony fingers gripped the arms of his chair.

'Why did you have to bring that up now? Just when I've told you I'm feeling better. Always wanting me in my grave, aren't you?'

He banged his fist again. 'I'll *not* alter my will, not until I'm on my death bed. It's tempting Providence, that's what it is. I'm not going to die yet. You said so yourself, the night Rosamund's portrait fell. It was Rosamund who died, not me. But she's come back. She's come back to me, just as she was as a little girl.'

'Then would it not be as well to provide for her future?' Jocelyn asked quietly.

Nathaniel glanced at her suspiciously. Then he pushed aside the rug covering his knees and rose unsteadily to his feet. Jocelyn moved to help him.

'Leave me alone! I can manage.'

He went to the window and stood looking out. She heard him muttering, but she could catch only a few words.

'Used to play in the garden . . . pretty girl . . . stay here, always . . . not go away.'

Jocelyn said cautiously, 'If you were to make over Penn Barton to Isabella, then you could be sure she never would go away.'

The old man was silent for a few minutes. Then he cackled. 'Yes, you're right. Even in my grave I'd know she was here, my pretty girl. I wouldn't be lonely, down in the cold earth. She'd bring me flowers and I'd know she was there, my little Isabella, my pretty Rosamund.'

Jocelyn pressed her advantage.

'Shall I ask Mr. Creedy to come up, to discuss the matter with you?'

'Discuss? Discuss? Why should I want to *discuss* it with him? I *tell* Creedy what to do, and he does it. I don't invite his opinion, I . . .' He turned and faced Jocelyn, and his eyes were hard and suspicious. 'Why are you so anxious I should change my will, for it won't be to your advantage? Don't tell me you are thinking only of that child. It's the boy you dote on, isn't it? What game are you playing, Jocelyn?'

'It's not a game, Grandfather. It would give me the greatest pleasure if you changed your will in favour of all three children. But, even if you single out Isabella, it would still please me greatly.'

'Now, why? Oh, I don't expect you to answer. But I'll find out. There's something going on behind my back, and I've a suspicion that tricky lawyer is concerned in it.' He rubbed his forehead. 'I can't think properly. I get muddled. You're against me, Jocelyn, you always have been.'

'I assure you . . .' she began, dismayed that she had apparently lost her advantage.

'You'll assure me nothing. You lie and deceive me all the time, you always have. But I'll show you, I'll show you.' He moved to the small table beside his chair. With surprising strength he sent the tray and its contents crashing to the floor. 'Bring me red meat,' he demanded. 'That will help me think clearly. Until I've discovered how you and that damned lawyer are cheating me, I'll do nothing. You may tell Creedy to go to the devil, and take you with him.' He grasped his stick and made to strike her. 'Get out! D'you hear me? Get out! I want Rosamund. She's the only one who cares a jot for me. Tell her to come at once. Tell her that her old grandfather wants her to come and comfort him. She'll come, my pretty Rosamund, she'll come.'

7

Jocelyn could not make up her mind. Twice, that Sunday evening, she put on her cloak, then took it off again. More than anything she wanted to go down to Martha's cottage, for Adam had told her he would wait there each evening in the hope that she would be able to join him. But if she did go, could she any longer keep silent over her betrothal to Thomas?

Into her mind, while she still hesitated, came Doctor Marsh's words: 'You would not understand my weaknesses because you have none, it seems.'

Even had it been true then, it certainly was not so now. Only too clearly she saw her present weakness. Desperately she wanted to be loved, to be held in Adam's arms, gaining strength and comfort from his nearness. She wanted to experience the kind of joy which love could bring, even if it should be only for a little while. Was that so very wicked, she asked herself. After all, she had given Adam no promise and she would not do so.

Her conscience told her that was only an excuse. The very fact that she had responded to his kisses with such warmth was surely enough to convince him that he might one day expect her to be his wife, without the need of a spoken promise.

But was there not a hope, however faint, that one day she might be free? If her grandfather changed his will in favour of the children, even in favour of Isabella, then surely Thomas Creedy would no longer desire to marry her? While there was that hope, would it not be foolish to prejudice her chance of happiness? And why make Adam share the uncertainty, when she could keep it to herself?

Her conscience told her this was cheating, that in true love there should be no secrets, that it was her duty to tell him the truth. Her fear of losing him urged her to hold back, to snatch what happiness she could, while she could.

It was duty of a different kind which made her suddenly decide to go. For surely she must warn Adam of the suspicions being built around him? She was sure he had nothing to hide. But she ought to tell him that some people were reading an ulterior motive into his interest in ships passing close to the coast, and that even his generous gesture in securing the release of the free-traders was suspect in some quarters.

She left word with Polly to inform her grandfather, should he ask for her, that she had gone to Martha's cottage to collect the eggs. As she walked down the valley, the sun was setting behind the western hill, leaving Penn Barton and most of the village in shadow. It shone brightly on Galliards, lighting up the windows so that they seemed on fire.

A man appeared on the terrace. Jocelyn stopped, thinking it must be Adam. Perhaps he had already been down to the cliff and, not finding her there, returned to Galliards to fetch his horse.

As if to confirm that idea, he walked along the terrace and went into the stable. But when he came out again, he was not leading a horse. He disappeared into the nearest barn, but emerged almost at once. He stood for a few minutes, looking around him, then strolled towards the circular stone dovecote and, after a moment's hesitation, went inside.

A ray of sunshine, slanting across the valley, shone fully on to the dovecote. When the man came out and was silhouetted against the grey stone, he seemed shorter than Adam. She realised, too, that his movements were slower.

She was about to continue down the valley when she saw something else which made her pause and catch her breath. Tethered to a tree at the end of the terrace was a grey horse, which, even at this distance, Jocelyn recognized. She had seen it only an hour since, trotting away from Penn Barton with Thomas Creedy on its back.

Scrambling over a field-gate, she ran through a meadow, then crossed the stream by stepping-stones. She followed the path she had taken three days ago in search of the children, up a steep bank beside a stream, over the stile into the copse. When she came in sight of the outbuildings, she paused to get her breath. She heard the rooks cawing in the elms, and a blackbird singing. Thomas's grey cob pawed the gravel impatiently. Then, from the nearest outhouse, a ramshackle barn half-covered in creepers and brambles, came Thomas's dry cough.

Jocelyn sought the cover of some bushes and waited. It would be useless to rush forward and confront Thomas, demanding to know what he was doing on Adam's property. She could best serve Adam, she thought, by keeping watch on the lawyer's movements.

Thomas emerged from the barn, dusting down his brown velvet suit. Jocelyn could not see his face, but he was rubbing his hands together with an air of satisfaction. He pulled out his watch and glanced at it, then walked quickly along the terrace and mounted his horse. In a few moments he had disappeared down the drive.

To Jocelyn there seemed only one explanation for his actions. He had decided, after all, to take the searching of Galliards into his own hands. His air of satisfaction suggested that, by some mischance, he had discovered something incriminating in the barn. He had probably ridden off now to fetch the Preventive Officer.

Hastily she climbed the stile and made her way across the rough field towards the outbuildings.

It was dark inside the old barn and she had to accustom her eyes to the dimness before she could make out any details clearly. It was just as she remembered it from childhood days. The roof beams were sagging, the walls bulging outwards. Ivy, thick with dust and cobwebs, grew through the cracks. The old cart was still there, resting lop-sidedly on its shafts, one wheel missing, its floor-boards littered with wisps of rotted hay. It was strange, she thought, that the villagers had not broken it up and carried it away for firewood. Perhaps fear of Sir John Peverell's ghost had kept them from doing so.

She looked more closely at the cart, then exclaimed with pleasure. There was a robin's nest built on the axle, almost in the place where she had discovered one all those years ago. She bent down and saw the bird, sitting tight on its eggs, watching her warily.

She backed away and stood looking around her, puzzled. What had Thomas found in here to cause him such evident satisfaction? It was obvious that nothing had been disturbed for years.

While she was trying to find an explanation, she heard hooves thudding on the hard ground behind the outbuildings. Her first thought was that Thomas had returned.

She glanced hastily round, seeking somewhere to hide. She crouched down in the darkest corner, behind the sagging door.

She heard the horse come round the end of the building and slither to a stop.

Then Adam called anxiously, 'Jocelyn, Jocelyn, where are you?'

She exclaimed in relief and ran outside. 'Here, Adam, I'm here.'

He came swiftly to her and took hold of her shoulders. 'What is it, my darling? The children? Do you want me to take them?'

When she did not answer at once, he gave her a little shake. 'Tell me, what is wrong? I was waiting for you on the cliff. When you did not come, I started making my way down. Then I caught sight of you, running across the meadow and making for the copse.'

'You saw me?'

'Of course. Why else do you think I am here? Now, tell me, how can I help you?'

There was concern in his eyes, his fingers dug into her shoulders in his anxiety.

'Oh, my dear,' she said, 'just for once I did not come to you for help.' She leaned against him, resting her cheek against his. 'This time, I was trying to help you.'

She felt him relax. But he still rattled off questions at her. 'Why should you think I need help? And what were you doing, hiding yourself away in this old barn?'

She put a finger over his lips. 'If you will give me a chance, I will explain. There was a man here, my grandfather's lawyer, walking around your property. I came to find out what he was doing.'

Adam listened with growing incredulity as Jocelyn told him what had happened. When she had finished, he asked, 'What concern is it of this lawyer whether I am a freetrader or not? What can he hope to gain by trumping up a false charge against me?'

Jocelyn averted her face. Now was certainly not the time to tell Adam the truth about Thomas Creedy.

'He displeased Grandfather,' she said in explanation. 'He wants to return to favour for—his own reasons. Because of this feud between your family and mine, Grandfather seeks a way to harm you. Mr. Creedy will do

145

anything in his power to help him.'

Adam looked contemptuous. 'So? I have an old man of eighty and an interfering lawyer to contend with. I'faith, I think I would sooner fight a French privateer. At least one is face to face with the enemy and it is an open, honest fight, not a hole-in-the-corner affair like this.'

'But Grandfather could be quite as dangerous. And Mr. Creedy is not a man to be lightly dismissed. Adam, what could he have found?'

'Nothing, of course. After you told me that Galliards had a reputation as a hiding-place for contraband, I made a thorough search of the house and outbuildings. There is no trace of disturbance, no sign of any earth having been newly dug, no floorboards taken up that I can see.'

'But he seemed so pleased with himself, as if he had found something which would incriminate you. Adam, have a look inside this barn. I could find nothing wrong, but you may discover something.'

She tried to lead him towards the barn, but he held her close.

'There is no need to be anxious, my darling. I am in no danger. A man faces enough of that at sea without deliberately courting trouble when he's on dry land. I have done nothing against the law and I can assure you that this lawyer did not find any contraband.'

'Then why . . . ?'

He cut short her question with a kiss.

'Jocelyn, you worry too much. If you are so anxious about imaginary dangers, how will you fare when I am at sea? Will you spend every night on your knees, praying for my safety? Will you never have a moment's peace until I return?'

Jocelyn hid her face against his chest. 'I—dare not even think of the future.'

'But you must,' he said, holding her close. 'You must set your sights on that horizon. One day, despite all that may happen in the meantime to keep us apart, we will reach it, together.'

She clung to him, ashamed of her weakness in still keeping from him the greatest obstacle in their path. When he tilted up her head and kissed her, not tenderly but with a passion which made her gasp, she knew she had gone too far in silence to turn back.

Nathaniel rose at his usual late hour on Monday morning, rang for Polly to help him dress, and announced his intention of going downstairs. Jocelyn's offer to assist him along the passage and down the stairs was brusquely brushed aside. Watching him anxiously from the hall, she saw that the hand which gripped the banister looked surprisingly strong. He did not stumble or falter. Isabella had indeed worked a miracle.

He seated himself before the fire in the library and sent for the child. She went running in to him, proudly showing off a doll which she had been dressing.

The old man peremptorily waved Jocelyn away. She went to the dining-room to make sure that everything was in order since it seemed likely he would take his meals there today.

But, almost immediately, Polly appeared to tell Jocelyn she was wanted in the library.

Jocelyn sighed. 'Do you know what he wants me for?'

The maid shook her head gloomily. 'I wouldn't think 'tis to give you a guinea, ma'am, by the look on his face.'

Jocelyn's heart sank as she went across the hall. It was too much to hope, she supposed, that things would continue as smoothly as they had done for the past three days.

She was hardly inside the room when Nathaniel shot a question at her.

'Who is Captain Peril?'

As Jocelyn hesitated, Isabella held out the doll to her. 'Tie that sash,' she ordered imperiously.

Jocelyn played for time. 'Please,' she reminded the child. 'When you ask people to do things for you, you should say "Please."'

'Stop playing the schoolma'am and answer my question,' Nathaniel snapped. 'Who is this Captain Peril?'

Isabella frowned at Jocelyn, then smiled sweetly at her great-grandfather. 'He's a nice man. He gave me a ride on his horse.'

'When was this?'

Jocelyn said quickly, 'How do you want the sash tied, Isabella?'

Nathaniel rapped his stick on the floor. 'Answer my question.'

Unperturbed by this show of impatience, Isabella glanced wickedly up at Jocelyn, then opened her eyes innocently as she turned to the old man.

'When we got off the wagon. I wanted to see the horse and Aunt Jocelyn wouldn't let me, and then Captain Peril came along and put me on the horse and then when we left the horse behind he carried me on his shoulders and I pretended *he* was a horse.'

The little girl paused for breath and to see the effect of her words. The old man's eyes narrowed, his lips became a thin line. He leaned forward and patted Isabella's shoulder.

'You're a good girl to tell me this. Now run along and ask cook to give you a sweetmeat, or whatever else you'd like to eat.'

Isabella sidled up to him and kissed him on the cheek. Then she stood before Jocelyn, holding out the doll.

'I want the sash tied in a bow, of course.'

She tossed her ringlets and flounced across the room.

At the door, she looked over her shoulder and her small face was a study of triumph.

'Little monkey,' Nathaniel said delightedly. 'I've got my pretty Rosamund back again, just the same, just the same.'

Jocelyn stood waiting, gripping the doll. Her grandfather's expression changed, his voice was harsh.

'Come here, where I can see you.'

Reluctantly she moved to face the light.

'Now, miss, will you kindly answer my question. Who is this man the child is prattling about?'

Jocelyn stared down at the floor. 'Someone who helped me,' she murmured.

'Someone who helped you,' Nathaniel repeated scornfully. 'And whose name is Captain Peril! A likely name! I am not so hard of hearing, Jocelyn, nor so senile that I cannot turn "Peril" into "Peverell."' He poked at her skirt with his stick. 'Look at me, and don't mumble. Am I right?'

'Yes, you are right,' she answered resignedly.

'So?' He folded his hands on the knob of his stick and leaned his chin on them. 'You have met this man, despite my expressly forbidding you to do so. What have you to say?'

She raised her head and spoke firmly. 'I met Captain Peverell by chance. On the first occasion I did not know who he was . . .'

'You mean that you spoke to a strange man?'

'I had to do so. He was sitting on the stile below Martha's cottage. I was forced to ask him to move in order that I might pass.'

'That was the first time, you say? How many times have you met him since then?'

'Several.' Suddenly, Jocelyn realised the absurdity of the situation. A woman of twenty-two, with a doll clutched in her hands, was standing before an old man of eighty, and submitting to a catechism on her conduct as if she was no older than Isabella.

She said rebelliously, 'There was no harm in it. Captain Peverell has shown me nothing but kindness.'

'Do you think I care a fig for how he behaved to you? He's a damned Cavalier!'

'He is nothing of the sort,' she protested impatiently. 'This is the eighteenth century. Your obsession with the Civil War is absurd!'

'How dare you speak to me like that?' The old man's eyes blazed at her. The knuckles of his thin fingers looked as if they might burst through the skin. 'You have always defied me, lied to me . . .'

'That is unfair, and you know it.'

He recoiled as if she had struck him. His eyes narrowed, became like small hard pebbles.

'This time you have gone too far,' he said viciously. 'Since, apparently, my orders carry no weight with you, I shall use other means to curb your wilfulness. Bring the boy here.'

'The boy?' she repeated dully.

'The boy you dote on, who you tell me is Rosamund's son, though he has the misfortune to look like you. Bring him here at once.'

'What do you want him for?' she asked suspiciously.

He rapped his stick on the floor. 'Do as I tell you, and don't ask questions, or it will be the worse for you—and him.'

Swiftly she sought to save the situation. 'Grandfather, I am sorry if . . .' she began.

He rose and went to the window, turning his back on her. He rapped his knuckles on the sill.

'Damned Cavaliers! I'll burn their house about their ears, that's what I'll do!'

Seeing that any attempt at placating him was useless, Jocelyn went in search of Paul. She found him helping the garden boy to tie up some straggling roses on the wall of the house. Calling him to follow her, she went into the herb garden, where it was quiet, and sat on the seat where she had opened the letter from Rosamund. Whatever her grandfather might be planning, she felt that her nephew must be warned.

She took hold of his hand. 'Paul, you are to come with me to the library. I do not know what Grandfather wants you for, but I have displeased him. It may be that—that he will still be angry. You must not be afraid. But try not to make him more angry. If he questions you, you must of course answer. But do not say any more than you need. Do you understand?'

He nodded silently. The anxious look had returned to his face and she was dismayed that she had been foolish enough to provoke her grandfather unnecessarily. It had been bad enough that he had discovered her association with Adam, without adding fuel to the fire by openly defying the old man. Had his fury been directed solely at her, she could have borne it, as she had for so many years. But now it seemed her punishment was somehow to involve Paul, and she was afraid.

She rose, and smiled at Paul, trying to hide her apprehension. 'Come then.'

Paul kept hold of her hand as they went into the house. She smiled at him again as they entered the library. He was trying his best to put on a brave face, but his fingers were gripping hers very hard.

The old man glared at them.

'Come and stand here, both of you. And let go of the boy's hand, Jocelyn, he's not a baby!'

Colouring, Paul immediately drew away from her and stood straight-backed, squaring his shoulders. He looked at the old man unflinchingly. Nathaniel pointed with his stick.

'Fetch me my Bible.'

Jocelyn caught her breath. Her grandfather repeated the order. Reluctantly she fetched the big, heavy book from the desk and laid it on the table beside him.

'Now,' Nathaniel said, with relish. 'Now, miss, I am going to be lenient. I am going to give you a choice. Isn't that generous of me?'

Jocelyn did not answer. Generosity had never played any part in her grandfather's character. It was useless to hope that Isabella's presence had changed that, except towards the little girl herself.

Nathaniel folded his hands on the knob of his stick. It was obvious he was enjoying himself. 'I will make the choice perfectly clear, Jocelyn. Either you swear never to speak to Captain Peverell again, or this boy leaves my house, today.'

Jocelyn cried out in dismay. 'How can you suggest such a thing? Paul has done you no harm. He is Rosamund's son, he has every right . . .'

'*Right?*' The old man's eyes blazed. 'How dare you speak like that to me? I warn you, Jocelyn . . .'

'Is there no end to your callousness?' she demanded bitterly. 'How *can* you be so cruel as to make such a threat, in front of a child of nine? If you thought it necessary to punish me, then you could have done so . . .'

'*Be quiet!*'

The wildness she dreaded was in his eyes. Paul took a step backwards.

'Leave us,' she said to him quietly. 'Go and find Martha.'

The boy looked up at her and shook his head. Nathaniel's lips curled derisively.

'You don't seem to be able to enforce obedience, do you?' he asked. 'The boy is right, of course. *I* give the orders in this house, not you. Now, come here, come closer. Have you made your choice?'

Jocelyn stood looking at him, and at the Bible. She

felt as if there was a heavy weight pressing on her.

She said wearily, 'You know perfectly well that I have no choice, any more than I had seven years ago.' She stretched out her hand and rested her fingers on the heavy book. 'What is it you want me to swear?'

Before Nathaniel could answer, Paul stepped forward, and clutched her arm.

'No, Aunt Jocelyn, no. I can go to Galliards. I can go to Captain Peverell.'

Tears welled up into Jocelyn's eyes. She put her hand over his, but she could not trust herself to speak.

The old man looked at her triumphantly.

In a voice she scarcely recognised as her own, Jocelyn said, 'Tell me what you want me to swear!'

Nathaniel gave a cackling laugh. 'You will say after me . . .'

Jocelyn's mind went back seven years, when in this very room he had said those same words. She had been fifteen, made to suffer for her sister's misdeed. Now she was a woman, but just as helpless through her love for Rosamund's son, and her resolve to protect him at all costs.

Slowly, she repeated her grandfather's words. 'I swear never to speak to Captain Peverell again.'

Suddenly, seeing the triumph on her grandfather's face, Jocelyn rebelled. She was helpless now, there was no doubt of it. But later, after the old man was dead . . . Adam was a wealthy man. He had offered to care for the children. He wanted her as his wife. She saw clearly what she had been blind to. She had only to tell Adam of the contract of marriage with Thomas Creedy and he would find a solution to that problem, as he did to all others. In any case, if Nathaniel did not change his will, and she was his beneficiary, why should she not offer Penn Barton Manor to Thomas? It was her dowry he wanted, not her. Given that, surely he would free her so that she could marry Adam.

She was surprised that she had not thought of this solution before. But there was one thing she must do now, if she was to live with her conscience. Her hand was still on the Bible. She repeated the oath: 'I swear never to speak to Captain Peverell again.' Then she added, under her breath, 'until Grandfather is dead.'

Jocelyn was standing by her open window, watching the last of the sun's rays light up the façade of Galliards, when there came a tap at the door, and Martha appeared. The old woman's back was bent, her steps dragged. Jocelyn helped her to a chair.

'I should not have asked you to go,' she said, remorsefully. 'It is too far for you now, to your cottage and back.'

Martha gave her a weary smile. 'My legs aren't as good as they used to be. 'Tisn't often I climb up that cliff path nowadays.'

'Let me get you a cordial,' Jocelyn offered, but Martha put a hand on her arm.

'Bide a while, Miss Jocelyn. Let me tell you first . . .'

'You saw Captain Peverell?' Jocelyn asked eagerly.

Martha nodded. 'Aye, I saw him. He was waiting near the cottage. A fine figure of a man he looked too, standing so straight with a telescope to his eye, just as if he was on his own quarter-deck. When he heard me coming, he turned round so quick and eager I knew 'twas you he was expecting.'

Jocelyn put her hands to her cheeks. 'You told him why I had not come?'

'Of course. *And* all about that wicked vow the master made you take. When I'd done, Captain Peverell gripped that telescope so hard I thought he'd break it in two.'

'And then?'

'He bade me go inside the cottage and sit down while he got over his anger. When he'd calmed down he was all concern for you, Miss Jocelyn. We talked, then, for a while. There's one thing I'm certain about. He won't let you go, my dear.'

'Surely he will accept that I *cannot* see him—for Paul's sake?'

'He'll do that. But sailors are patient men, Miss Jocelyn, they've need to be. And they're used to being parted from their womenfolk for long spells at a time. He'll wait for you, however long, no fear of that.'

'But if he should wait in vain? Oh, Martha, I am wronging him so in not telling him about my betrothal.'

The old woman shook her head vehemently. ''Tis no use meeting that obstacle before it's necessary. And when it comes, I'd leave it to Captain Peverell to deal with. I reckon I know as what he'll do.'

Jocelyn went on her knees and took hold of Martha's wrinkled hands. 'What will he do? Tell me, if you think it holds out any hope.'

The old woman smiled down at her. 'Why, my dear, he'll kidnap you, you and the children, and carry you off in one of his ships, and have a wedding ring on your finger before that dry stick of a lawyer has mounted his horse to come and collect your dowry.'

Jocelyn laid her head on Martha's knee. 'If only that could be so. For then I should not be breaking any contract. I could scarcely pit my strength against a merchant captain's, could I—not if he carried me off by force?'

She sat back on her heels. 'But let us be sensible. Did he give you any message for me?'

'Yes, indeed. I was telling him what a fine view there was of his house from your bedroom window. He says he's sleeping at Galliards tonight.'

'I did not think it was ready for occupation.'

'He says he can manage with few comforts, and after what you told him last evening he prefers to be there at night in case the Preventive Officer decides to pay a secret visit. What I had to tell you was that he will put a lighted lantern in the window above the porch each evening so that you will know that he is there and thinking about you.'

Jocelyn rose and went swiftly to the window.

''Twill not be there yet, my dear, I think. I left him on the cliff, staring out to sea. He'd a lot of thinking to do, I reckon.'

Jocelyn sighed, then, noticing again how weary Martha looked, said decisively, 'Now I *will* get you some cordial. You are to sit here and rest while I go and fetch it. And thank you, Martha. You are the only person I could trust to explain to Captain Peverell why I cannot—cannot . . .' She hurried from the room, fighting back her tears.

Determinedly, Jocelyn schooled herself to live each day at a time. She worked out a time-table which would leave her little opportunity for brooding or self-pity. In the mornings, before Nathaniel rose, she gave the two older children lessons. During these, Isabella was no trouble at all, and Jocelyn grew a great deal fonder of the child. To Jocelyn's surprise the little girl, unlike her mother, showed an aptitude and eagerness to learn. Paul applied himself to his books with the same concentration with which he did every task. Jocelyn found these hours enjoyable and rewarding. She was still unsure of herself with the baby, but Martha happily took charge of Sarah.

Once Nathaniel was dressed, he claimed Isabella for himself and sent for her to join him in the library. Jocelyn then carried out her usual household duties while Paul helped the garden-boy. In the afternoon, with the little girl closeted with the old man, Jocelyn took Paul for a walk or gave him a lesson in riding her pony. Isabella's desire to be included in the latter pastime was denied her by her great-grandfather. No cajoling or show of tantrums on her part would move him an inch from this decision. Jocelyn could guess the reason. He was remembering that his grandson William had been killed by a fall from his pony when only thirteen years old. Jocelyn could not help feeling a little sorry for Isabella. To ride a horse was the height of her desire. To be thwarted in this by the person who appeared to grant her every wish, was beyond the child's understanding.

Despite her anxiety regarding the future, Jocelyn decided against reminding her grandfather about the question of changing his will. An opportunity might present itself on Sunday, when Thomas paid his weekly visit to Penn Barton. She might have a chance then, also, of questioning Thomas guardedly about what he had been doing at Galliards.

She viewed this coming Sunday with mixed feelings. For one thing it would mean she would see Adam at church. She longed for even a sight of him, yet knew that if her grandfather should be so improved he decided to attend, she would not dare even to cast a glance in Adam's direction.

The week passed. There was rain, two days of cold wind which coincided with the full moon, then a calm Friday with a return of warmth and sunshine.

In the afternoon, returning from a walk with Paul, Jocelyn saw, to her surprise, the doctor's horse tethered at the gate. She hurried in, fearful lest Nathaniel had been taken ill again. But Polly assured her that he was, if anything, stronger, although he seemed rather excited.

The maid's freckled face was flushed, her eyes bright. She drew Jocelyn aside, out of Paul's hearing.

'There be summat strange going on, ma'am, I'm thinking. The master sent the garden boy with a note to the doctor, and he came at once though there seemed no call for haste. After he'd been here a while, cook was sent for, but she won't tell why. She says the master swore her to secrecy on pain of instant dismissal.' Polly's eyes grew big, her voice full of awe. 'Whatever d'you suppose is going on, ma'am?'

'I have no idea,' Jocelyn told her. 'And I must remind you, Polly, that whatever it is, it is no concern of yours.'

Nor did it seem that she herself was to be given any explanation. While she was changing her gown, Jocelyn heard the doctor's horse trot away. Not once during the rest of the day did her grandfather refer to Doctor Marsh's visit, nor offer any enlightenment as to why he had been sent for.

That night, Jocelyn had a disturbing dream. Thomas Creedy was leaning over her, shaking her into wakefulness. She shrank away, hunching up her shoulder. The shaking continued, more vigorously.

A voice demanded urgently, 'Aunt Jocelyn, wake up!'

She became aware that the hand shaking her shoulder was real. So, too, was the voice. She opened her eyes. The room was bathed in moonlight.

The voice persisted.

'Aunt Jocelyn, please wake up properly, and listen to me.'

'Paul?'

Jocelyn sat up, rubbing her eyes. The boy was dressed only in his nightshirt, his hair falling over his forehead. 'What is it?' she asked anxiously. 'Paul, what's the matter? Are you unwell?'

'No. But I must talk to you. Are you listening?'

'Yes.'

She heard an odd sound and realised it was Paul's teeth chattering. She felt his hands.

'Darling, you're so cold.' She pushed down the coverlet. 'Come under here and get warm.'

He clambered on to the bed and she wrapped him

round with the coverlet. 'How did you get so cold?'

'I was standing at the window, hoping to see the smugglers.'

'Oh, Paul! They wouldn't be out on such a moonlit night. They bring their goods ashore when it is very dark.'

His teeth were still chattering and he was shivering. Jocelyn realised suddenly that it was not only because of cold. She put an arm about him.

'Something has frightened you. What is it?'

'I saw . . . I saw great-grandfather in the garden.'

She exclaimed in relief. 'You've been dreaming!'

He shook his head vehemently. 'No. It wasn't a dream.'

'What would he be doing in the garden, in the middle of the night?'

'I don't know, but . . .'

She ran her fingers through his hair. 'I was dreaming, too, when you woke me. All sorts of strange things happen in dreams.'

He pulled away from her and repeated earnestly, 'Aunt Jocelyn, it *wasn't* a dream. I saw him. He went along the path and out of the gate. I heard it squeak. He had his coat and hat on. He was leaning on a stick and talking to himself.'

She let him continue. Her own dream had been very real.

'He was saying—Aunt Jocelyn, are you listening to me?'

'Yes, dear, I'm listening,' she said soothingly.

'He was saying, quite loudly, "I'll burn their house about their ears, the damned Cavaliers."'

She could not help smiling. The dream had indeed been realistic.

Paul shook her arm. 'You've got to believe me. It *was* him, and he *did* say that, and he *has* gone out of the gate. I—I went to his bedroom.'

'You did—*what?*'

'I tiptoed down to his bedroom and looked round the door. The candle was still burning, but he wasn't there. The bed was empty.'

Jocelyn grasped his arm. 'Paul, what are you saying?'

His voice was squeaky with excitement. 'It's *true*, Aunt Jocelyn. If you come with me I'll show you.'

She slid out of bed and flung her wrapper about her shoulders. Paul freed himself from the coverlet. Together they went along the moonlit passage. Jocelyn paused in the doorway of Nathaniel's room. Candlelight shone faintly on the closed shutters. She glanced down at her nephew. He nodded eagerly, and tugged at her hand.

Holding her breath, she peered round the door. The bed was empty. There was no one in the room.

'Now will you believe it wasn't a dream?' Paul demanded.

She did not answer, but went quickly to the closet where her grandfather kept his clothes. His black suit that he wore every day was missing, and his hat from the shelf above. His slippers were beside the bed, his nightcap on the floor. Still she could not believe what the boy had told her.

'Let us go up to your room, Paul.'

When they reached it she felt the chill breeze from the open window penetrate her thin wrapper. She took Paul's coat from off its peg and put it around his shoulders.

'Show me where you were watching from.'

He took his position, kneeling on the window-sill. His eyes, in the bright light of the moon, looked big and dark against the paleness of his face. She knelt beside him and peered out. The path below was clearly visible, and the gate in the high wall. She saw that it was ajar. Something moved in the bushes, the sound very loud in the silent night. It was perfectly possible, she realised, for Paul to have heard, as well as seen, anyone on the path below.

Yet the boy's story was ridiculous, impossible. Nathaniel was stronger, certainly, but he had not yet ventured out of doors. What madness had possessed him to dress himself and go out, alone, into the night?

'What did you hear him say?' she asked Paul.

He repeated it excitedly. ' "I'll burn their house about their ears, the damned Cavaliers!" '

Jocelyn realised then what had lent the old man strength—his hatred of the Peverells.

She became aware that Paul was watching her intently. In an awed voice, he asked, 'Will you go after him?'

His words jolted her into action. She rose from the window-sill. 'Yes. Yes, of course.'

'I shall come with you,' he declared, standing very straight before her.

She put a hand on his shoulder. 'Darling, no. You are only a little boy.'

Immediately, as she saw the hurt in his eyes, she regretted her words. He thrust up his chin.

'Captain Peverell doesn't think I'm a little boy. He said I was to look after you.'

Jocelyn hesitated. How could she take a child on a mission she herself dreaded? Yet, if she refused him, it would be a dreadful blow to his pride, and he had been hurt enough already.

'Very well,' she agreed with some reluctance. 'But you must promise to do exactly as I tell you. If, when we find grandfather, he becomes angry, you are to keep out of sight. Will you promise that?'

He nodded eagerly. 'Shall we take a pistol?'

'A pistol?' she repeated, horrified. 'Whatever for?'

'In case we meet a smuggler.'

She was about to repeat her statement that it was far

too light a night for the freetraders to be about. Then she saw that to Paul, this was simply an adventure. He had no idea of how grave the consequences might be.

'No, I do not think we should take a pistol,' she said. 'But you may carry my riding-whip if you wish. Dress yourself quickly.'

To save time she put on her riding-habit and boots. When Paul joined her, they tiptoed down the stairs and let themselves out of the side door, then went quietly along the path and down the steps. Jocelyn paused, wondering whether her grandfather had gone through the village or by a field path which skirted it. She listened for the sound of a dog barking which might indicate his route. There was silence save for an owl hooting and the ripple of the stream. Paul, gripping her whip, kept very close.

'Isn't it mysterious?' he whispered. 'I've never been out in the middle of the night before.'

'I have,' she said reassuringly. 'Though it was a long time ago.'

She chose the path which led through the fields. It was no use attempting the short cut by the smugglers' path at night, even on one as bright as this. But she did not want anyone in the village to hear them and perhaps open a window and ask who was about.

The grass was long and wet, and she was glad of her high boots. The hedges of hawthorn gleamed whitely, and their scent was almost cloying in its sweetness. A barn owl flew from an elm tree. In the bright light, they could see its head turning from side to side as it searched for mice and voles. The night was so still and quiet that Jocelyn could hear the waves breaking on the shingle beach almost a mile away.

Suddenly Paul grasped her arm. 'Aunt Jocelyn, look.'

He was pointing ahead of them. The façade of Galliards was half in shadow, but moonlight fell full upon the terrace. A small dark figure was silhouetted there.

Jocelyn exclaimed in dismay, 'He can't have . . . He *can't* have . . .' As if to refute her words, she saw a stick raised and shaken in an angry gesture.

'Paul, we must get to him!'

Gathering up the thick folds of her habit, she began to run. The ground was uneven and she stumbled in her haste. She was slower than Paul at climbing a field gate and he raced ahead of her.

'Wait for me! Paul, wait for me!' she called after him.

Heedless of her warning, the boy ran on. The ground sloped uphill now, and Jocelyn was losing her breath. Twice she was forced to stop, as a stitch in her side nearly doubled her up. At last she reached the drive, where the going was easier.

Paul, ahead of her, was shouting, 'Captain Peverell! Captain Peverell!'

When Jocelyn caught up with him on the terrace, he was jumping up and down with excitement.

'That way, Aunt Jocelyn, that way!' His voice was shrill as he pointed towards the stables. 'He's got a tinder-box. I saw it.'

Again he shouted Adam's name, calling for help at the top of his voice. Jocelyn ran along the terrace. With dismay, she remembered that just inside the stable door was the pile of hay Adam had pulled down for them to sit on.

When she reached the old man, he was tugging at the hay, muttering to himself. She heard a rasping noise. A flicker of flame showed between Nathaniel's hands.

Jocelyn snatched at the tinder-box.

'No, Grandfather. No!'

Nathaniel brandished his stick. 'Keep away. I said I'd do it and I will. I'll burn down their house, the damned Cavaliers!'

He lashed out at her: then with a startled cry he

staggered backwards, dropping the tinder-box. He began to retreat, holding out his hands as if to fend off an enemy. There was a look of horror on his face. Jocelyn realised that he was staring at something behind her. She turned, and gasped at what she saw.

On the balustrade, silhouetted against the dark trees of the wood, was the figure of a man. He was dressed in white frilled shirt and pale-coloured breeches. His hair fell loose about his shoulders. There was a sword in his hand.

Nathaniel uttered a despairing cry. He clutched his throat.

'Don't come near me! Don't come near me, d'you hear?'

Jocelyn reached him as he stumbled. His stick clattered on the gravel. She heard someone running towards them. Her grandfather clutched at her arm.

'Save me! Save me, Jocelyn! It's the ghost, it's . . .'

His words ended on a wail. He fell against her and his weight carried her to the ground with him.

The next moment, Adam was kneeling beside her. Swiftly he unbuttoned Nathaniel's coat and put his ear to the old man's heart. After a moment or two, he raised his head. Jocelyn's eyes met his.

'Is he . . . ?' She could not bring herself to speak the words.

Adam nodded. 'He is dead. This is your grandfather?'

'Yes.' She could not really take in what he had said. 'He—he came to burn down your house.'

A sound behind her made her turn. Paul was standing a few feet away, staring at the little group. Jocelyn held out her hand. Paul ran to her and hid his face against her shoulder.

'Darling, I'm sorry,' she said, her voice trembling. 'I should not have let you come, not to see—this.'

'But what happened?' Adam asked. 'I did not even touch him, and yet . . .'

'Did you not hear what he said? He thought you were John Peverell's ghost, come out of the woods. I can understand that. Just for a moment, in the moonlight, you looked . . .' She broke off, and began to tremble. 'Oh, Adam.'

'You could not have saved him, Jocelyn,' he said. 'He killed himself, by his hatred of the Peverells.' Gently he helped her to her feet. He put an arm around her waist, the other around Paul's shoulders, enclosing them in a little circle of strength and security.

'It's ended, Jocelyn,' he said quietly. 'All the years of unhappiness and loneliness are over. You're free, my darling, you're free.'

8

Adam carried Nathaniel home and laid him on his bed, then went for the doctor. It was the first time in over a hundred years that a Peverell had set foot in Penn Barton Manor. Jocelyn almost expected her grandfather to rise from his bed and shake his fist at such an outrage.

But he lay still and peaceful, as he had never done in life. The doctor came, then the parson. A few villagers called. Jocelyn sent the garden boy on her pony with a note for Thomas Creedy. She took from its moth-balls the black velvet dress she had worn when her father died, and found that it needed little alteration. She set Polly to work on it, and in the meantime put on the dark silk she wore on Sundays and dressed her hair plainly in a coil on the nape of her neck.

With the shutters closed tightly over every window, the rooms were gloomier than ever and unbearably stuffy. The servants spoke in hushed voices and walked on tiptoe. The anxiety had returned to Paul's face. Isabella was tearful.

By mid-morning, Jocelyn could no longer bear to be inside the house. She went into the herb garden and paced restlessly up and down, longing for, and yet dreading, Adam's coming. She knew a moment of panic when she saw him ride up to the gate quite openly; then remembered that there was no longer need for secrecy. He caught sight of her through the gap in the wall, and came striding along the path. Tossing his hat on the seat, he held out his arms.

When she made no move to go to him, he regarded

her with a puzzled expression.

'What is it, my love? Has something happened to distress you further?'

Jocelyn hesitated. Although she had been rehearsing the words she would use, now that the time had come, she could not bring herself to say them.

He came close and took hold of her hands. 'Should I have come earlier? I would have done so, had I thought that was what you wanted. But it seemed to me that until you were alone, it was best to stay away. My presence here would have called for an explanation which would have embarrassed you.' He gave her hand a little shake. 'Jocelyn, are you listening to me?'

She nodded, but still she could not bring herself to speak. Adam put an arm around her shoulders.

'I understand. There is no need to pretend to me that you feel any grief, but you have had a great shock. Come, let us sit together and talk of happier times.'

With his arm about her, his voice warm and caressing in her ears, Jocelyn felt herself weakening yet again. She recalled the words of Doctor Marsh: 'Once you give way to weakness, it takes a hold on you.'

How true that was. Yet she had despised the doctor for *his* weakness.

Abruptly she freed herself from Adam's arm and turned to face him.

'Adam, listen, please listen. There is something I must tell you. I ought to have told you before. I have been very unfair to you, but I wanted . . .'

She broke off at the sound of hooves coming up the lane. Adam frowned and glanced over his shoulder.

'Who is it this time?' he asked with a note of exasperation in his voice.

Jocelyn's heart sank. 'It will, I think, be grandfather's lawyer.'

'The fellow who came prying round Galliards last

Sunday? I shall derive great pleasure from asking him what the devil he meant by it.'

Jocelyn clutched at his arm. 'Adam, please go. Please leave me alone with Mr. Creedy. There is something you must hear, but you must hear it only from me. Oh, why did I not tell you before?'

Adam stood his ground, looking from Jocelyn to the black-garbed figure of the lawyer approaching along the garden path.

Thomas caught sight of them and raised his hat.

He said unctuously, 'Miss Jocelyn, I came as soon as I received your note. This must have been a great shock to you. I offer my condolences, and any assistance I can render you.' He glanced pointedly at Adam. 'I think I have not the pleasure . . .'

Jocelyn siad reluctantly, 'This is Captain Peverell of Galliards. Mr. Thomas Creedy from Honiton, my grandfather's lawyer.'

Adam's greeting was scarcely more than a nod. Thomas stared at him in astonishment.

'Captain Peverell *here?* Miss Jocelyn, this is beyond my comprehension. If Mr. Harmer had even suspected you were acquainted . . .'

'He knew about it,' Adam said grimly. 'He forbade us to meet. But he is no longer alive. So I came, to claim my right . . .'

'Your *right?* Have you taken leave of your senses, sir? You have no right even to be on Mr. Harmer's property.'

'Since I assume Miss Harmer is now the mistress of it,' Adam retorted coolly, 'surely that is for her to say.' He turned expectantly to Jocelyn.

She made an effort to control her voice, but her words came out tense and clipped. 'Please—leave us, Adam. There are certain matters I must discuss with Mr. Creedy —certain private matters, which concern him very closely.'

To Jocelyn's relief, he appeared to accept her explanation.

'Very well,' he said, shrugging, 'if that is what you wish. I will return later to hear what you have to tell me, though I cannot suppose it is such a grave matter as you implied.'

Thomas drew himself up. 'You will certainly not return later, sir.'

Adam, from his greater height, looked down on the lawyer. 'Are *you* going to stop me?'

Jocelyn stepped forward, but Adam stretched out his hand warningly.

'There is no need for you to be concerned in this argument, Jocelyn. I can deal with Mr. Creedy. Moreover, since he has chosen to bring up the subject of right of entry upon private property, I shall ask him . . .' He broke off, frowning. 'But no, this is not the time.'

He picked up his hat from the seat. 'Do not weary Miss Harmer with too much legal talk, Mr. Creedy. As you remarked, she has had a great shock. She needs rest and quiet.'

Thomas's tone was icy. 'I really think, sir, that I may be allowed to know what is best for my future wife.'

Adam, about to pass him, stopped abruptly. 'What was that?'

Jocelyn ran forward and gave him a push. 'Adam, please go.'

He looked at her, a long, searching look, then turned to Thomas. 'Will you have the goodness to repeat your words?' he asked.

As Thomas did so, Jocelyn put her hands to her cheeks. Adam took hold of them roughly and forced her to look at him.

'Is this true? Is this what you had to tell me?'

'Yes,' she said helplessly. 'I—Adam, you do not understand.'

'Indeed, you are right,' he said grimly. 'How long have you been betrothed to this—this *gentleman?*' His tone was cutting, and Thomas started to protest. Adam turned on him angrily. 'I am not addressing you, sir. Jocelyn, answer me. How long?'

'Quite a long while. It was Grandfather's wish. He—he made a contract of marriage between Mr. Creedy and me. I—was forced to sign it.' The expression on Adam's face frightened her. 'Please,' she pleaded, 'try to understand.'

'I understand perfectly,' he said, and his voice was as hard as his eyes. 'I have been very useful to you, have I not? Though why you could not call upon your fiancé to assist you in the matter of the children, I cannot imagine. But then,' he added, 'he lives at Honiton, you said, so presumably he could not so easily be called upon.'

He stood close to her and spoke very low. His face looked drawn and his tone was so bitter that she knew how deeply she had hurt him.

'I thought you alone and helpless, I thought you depended on me, called upon me because you had no one else. But all the time . . .'

'Captain Peverell,' Thomas interrupted sharply. 'I really must protest. You are greatly distressing Miss Harner. Surely you can see that?'

'Oh, yes. I can see that,' Adam declared scornfully. 'As to my feelings . . .' He gave a mirthless laugh. 'The first time we met, Miss Harner, the cuckoo called. How very right he was.'

He rammed on his hat and walked swiftly along the path and slammed the gate behind him. To Jocelyn, the pounding of his horse's hooves down the lane sounded the end of hope.

She became aware that Thomas was talking, but she found it impossible to concentrate on what he was saying.

When he took hold of her arm and attempted to lead her to the house, she shrank away from his touch.

He said, in an offended tone, 'I am doing my best to make allowances for your conduct, Jocelyn, but I really must protest at this unseemly behaviour.'

It was the first time he had used her Christian name without the prefix. She realised that he was already anticipating their marriage and the time when he would have power over her. She felt a sudden flare-up of rebelliousness.

She said coldly, 'Mr. Creedy, you are not yet my husband. Until that time, I shall behave exactly as I wish. And now, if you will come into the library, I will tell you what arrangements have been made for the burial. It is to be this evening. The doctor and the parson have been very kind and helpful.'

'I should have thought,' Thomas remarked coldly, 'that it was my prerogative to . . .'

'Possibly. But I was not to know that you would come so speedily.'

Her tone was sarcastic. It was a relief to vent upon Thomas some of the bitterness she was feeling. Added to her own despair was the realisation of the hurt she had dealt Adam. He had not failed to come when she needed him, not once. She had rewarded him with utter rejection, and the knowledge that she had cheated him. That she had not actually lied to him was of no consequence. Her silence had been equally unforgiveable.

She went with Thomas into the gloomy library. As soon as they sat down, he drew a document from his pocket.

'This is Mr. Harmer's will. You are, I believe, aware of its contents. But, for the sake of formality, I will repeat the main clauses. You are Mr. Harmer's sole beneficiary, subject to my administration of the estate. When our marriage takes place, all money and this property will, of course, pass into my hands.'

His words seemed to her like a door being shut, firmly and irrevocably. Desperately, she sought to escape.

'If I were to ask you to release me from this contract of marriage—if I offered you Penn Barton, a sum of money, all I have . . .'

Even in the subdued light, she could see the expression of horror on Thomas's face.

'Are you out of your mind?' he demanded. 'There can be no question of breaking the contract.'

'But you do not want *me*,' she argued.

'Miss Jocelyn, I assure you, I have the greatest regard for you.'

'But even more for my dowry.'

She had not meant to say it. Yet she felt relief that she had done so. Now there could be no more pretence between them.

Thomas rose to his feet and looked down at her. 'I think you do not realise quite how offensive that remark was. I have never denied that your dowry would be—most welcome. As you must be aware, Mr. Harmer owes me a considerable amount of money for the law suits I have undertaken for him.'

'The estate would more than settle that,' she pointed out eagerly. 'Mr. Creedy, I beg you to be honest with yourself and with me.'

'Very well, then.' His tone, and the expression in his pale eyes, made Jocelyn wonder if she had gone too far. 'Since you seem determined to insult me—and I cannot think that I have ever given you cause to do so—I will speak plainly. I am a man of some position and reputation in Honiton. If our marriage did not take place, I should suffer the greatest indignity. And that, I am *not* prepared to tolerate.'

Jocelyn knew herself beaten. She was as powerless to

alter her future as she had been before her grandfather's death.

She raised her head and said wearily, 'There is the question of the children.'

Thomas regarded her coldly. 'As to that . . .'

He broke off, frowning, at a loud rap on the door. It opened immediately to reveal the burly figure of Doctor Marsh, thrusting Polly aside.

'I meant to come as soon as I saw your lawyer's horse at the gate, Miss Harmer,' he said, with a brusque nod towards Thomas. 'But I've been delayed with a sick child.'

Thomas asked disdainfully, 'May I ask what brings you here in such haste, without even waiting to be announced?'

The doctor eyed him up and down. 'You may not. I don't have to answer to you for my conduct, and as Miss Harmer has always had a poor opinion of me . . .'

'That is not true,' Jocelyn protested. 'As a physician . . .'

'Ah, yes, I had forgotten. You hold my professional skill in high esteem, but as a man you consider me a weakling and a ne'er-do-well.' He came to her side. 'You may not believe it, but yesterday I tried to act for your good. I tried to stop that old scoundrel from dealing you yet another blow.' He looked round hopefully. 'As your physician, Miss Harmer, I would recommend you to take a glass of wine. As the bringer of bad news, I would greatly appreciate one.'

'Bad news?' she repeated, at a loss. 'What kind of bad news?'

'The kind that will be no better or worse for keeping until my throat is less parched.' He reached out his hand towards the bell-rope. 'May I ring for your maid to bring some wine?'

While Polly served them, Thomas sat stiff-kneed and tight-lipped. The doctor sprawled in a leather chair. Jocelyn suddenly saw Doctor Marsh in a different light.

Beside the cold, egotistical lawyer, he seemed to her now intensely human. True, there was his weakness for drink. But she had never known it to interfere with his care of the sick of the parish. In any case, it was not for her to judge him. His weakness affected nobody but himself, whereas she had succumbed to one which had deeply hurt the man she loved.

When Polly left them, the physician drained his glass and banged it down so hard that Jocelyn feared it would break. Then he took a paper from his pocket and thrust it towards Thomas.

'Read that.'

Thomas regarded the document with distaste. 'Sir, I must ...'

'Read it, I say,' the doctor insisted. 'I was supposed to hand it to you tomorrow, when you arrived for your Sunday junketing. In the changed circumstances, it's my duty to give it to you now. Though I don't mind telling you I'd a mind to destroy it, seeing what further burdens the old devil thought up to lay upon his granddaughter's shoulders.' He turned to Jocelyn. 'I thought, when he died, you'd be free. I thought you'd inherit this property, be your own mistress, choose a husband if you'd a mind to.'

Jocelyn lowered her eyes. Thomas cleared his throat. 'Doctor Marsh, I think I should inform you ...' he began in his most precise tone.

The doctor tapped the document he had given the lawyer. 'You read that before you inform me of anything.' He leaned forward. 'Tell me, did you ever know a man to make a new will the very day he died?'

Thomas shot up in his chair as if he had been stung. '*What?* What did you say?'

Jocelyn stared at the doctor, as startled as Thomas at the question.

'A new will?' she repeated. 'Is that what ...?' She

175

gestured vaguely towards the document in Thomas's hands.

'Aye, that's what it is,' Doctor Marsh declared angrily. 'The old man called me in here yesterday. I had to come like a thief in the night, when you were out, and I don't wonder.'

Thomas's face had gone very pale. His fingers trembled as he unfolded the paper. Jocelyn waited, tense and silent, while he read through it.

The doctor helped himself to more wine. 'I suppose it's legal?' he asked. 'The old devil seemed to think so.'

In a strained voice, Thomas asked, 'Whose is the second signature? It is an uneducated hand, scarcely legible.'

'The cook's. She signed it willingly enough. Though I doubt she would have done so if she'd known how it would affect Miss Harmer.'

Jocelyn clasped her hands tightly together. 'May I be allowed to know the contents, Mr. Creedy?'

Thomas's lips were working. The paper shook between his thin fingers. He began to read.

'I, *Nathaniel Edmund Harmer, being in my right mind* . . .' He broke off. '*That* I should very much doubt. Doctor Marsh, surely as Mr. Harmer's physician . . .'

The doctor shook his head. 'He'd queer ways, of course, and his temper was enough to scare an army. But I can't truthfully say that . . .'

Jocelyn thumped her clenched fist on the arm of her chair. 'Will you please read that will? Don't bother with the preliminaries. Just tell me what changes he made.'

Thomas cleared his throat. 'What it amounts to, is that he has left his entire property to his great-granddaugther, Isabella.'

Jocelyn put her hands to her mouth to stifle her exclamation of joy. Misinterpreting her reaction, Doctor Marsh leaned towards her.

'I'm sorry, Miss Jocelyn, truly I am. I did my best . . .'

'Yes, I am sure you did,' she said impatiently. 'Pray go on, Mr. Creedy.'

He looked at her reproachfully. 'You do not seem to realise how painful this is to me. That Mr. Harmer should . . .'

'Get on man, get on,' the doctor urged. 'Tell Miss Harmer how she's tied to the child, the same way that she was tied to the old man for years.'

'That is true.' Thomas glanced at Jocelyn. 'He has appointed you her guardian, to remain with her as long as she needs you.'

Jocelyn tried hard to hide her relief. 'And the other children?' she asked.

'They are not mentioned. Neither, save for a paltry sum which will scarcely cover my fees over the past few months, am I.'

Jocelyn closed her eyes, gripping the arms of her chair. She scarcely dare let herself believe what she had heard. The doctor laid a hand on her arm. His voice was rough with sympathy.

'There was nothing I could do to stop him—nothing.'

She opened her eyes and smiled at him; then stretched out her hand.

'May I see the new will for myself, please?'

Reluctantly Thomas passed her the document. She read it through quickly, then raised her head.

'Doctor Marsh, I appreciate your kindness in trying to persuade Grandfather not to leave his property away from me. But, I do assure you, this change does not cause me any real distress. I am very fond of my niece Isabella. I am sure that, when she is old enough to understand the situation, she will wish to make provision for her younger sister, and to give her brother any help he may need.'

He stared at her in astonishment. 'But you're *tied*,' he declared. 'You're tied hand and foot, just as you've been for years.'

She shook her head. 'No,' she said, and smiled to herself. 'I think not.'

She rose and held out her hand. 'Perhaps you will come to see me again, Doctor Marsh, after the funeral? I think we may begin to understand each other a little better, now.'

As he took her hand, he looked at her with puzzled eyes. It was obvious he did not understand the situation in the least, and was loath to leave.

'I will come tonight,' he said. 'It is possible you may be feeling rather low then and need a draught to help you sleep.'

When the door had closed behind him, Thomas exclaimed, with more vigour than Jocelyn had ever heard in his voice, 'It's dastardly! After all I've done for your grandfather!'

Jocelyn looked at him calmly. It must be a great disappointment to you. It seems that if I become your wife I should bring you no dowry. Also, naturally, I shall be under an obligation to care for Isabella. And, as I have already told you, I hold myself responsible for the two other children.'

She waited, feeling a sense of triumph at his discomfiture.

He said, at last, 'As I think you must realise, this alters the situation.'

'So much, in fact, that you would like to change your mind? I assure you, I should not hold it against you. As to any indignity you may suffer, surely my grandfather can be held wholly to blame for our marriage not taking place? You could, perhaps, say that he tore up the contract in a fit of temper? That would save your reputation, would it not?'

His pale eyes were expressionless, his hands hanging limply between his knees. She could even find it in her heart to feel sorry for him.

She said quietly, 'You will realise, I am sure, that it would not be seemly for me to invite you to stay for dinner. The inn on the highway, I believe, is very well appointed.'

She went with him to the door. From across the valley came the faint sound of hammering.

Thomas frowned. 'That should be enough to make your grandfather rise from his death-bed.'

'It was his obsession with that old quarrel which laid him there,' Jocelyn remarked bitterly.

'And quite unnecessarily. There was no need for him to take upon himself the means of harming Captain Peverell. I was on the point of carrying out his wishes, making a case . . .'

'Against Captain Peverell? How could you do that? He is in no way involved with the freetraders.'

He looked at her with malice. 'Are you so sure? He was very hasty to pay fines imposed on notorious smugglers. He bribed a magistrate, kept a lantern burning in an upstairs window.'

'How do you know that?' Jocelyn demanded sharply.

'I have my informants, just as the Preventive Officer has. However . . .'

Thomas put on his hat and started down the path. Jocelyn ran after him and clutched at his arm.

'What have you done? What trick have you played? I saw you at Galliards, poking and prying around the outbuildings. I saw you come out of the barn.'

He glanced at her, startled, then lowered his eyes. It was obvious she had caught him off his guard. She shook his arm.

'What were you doing there?' she demanded.

Thomas quickly recovered his self-assurance. 'Searching for contraband, naturally.'

'But you did not find any. You could not have done. I looked around the barn after you had gone.'

179

He smiled frostily. 'Then you had better look again—except that it might be too late.'

'What do you mean?'

He pushed her hand from his arm. 'I have grown tired of this cross-examination, ma'am. Since you appear to be so well acquainted with Captain Peverell, doubtless you will learn, in due course, that he is not as innocent as you suppose. I bid you good-day.'

After he had gone, Jocelyn stood staring across the valley. Everything that had happened seemed suddenly unreal: the quiet, shuttered house, the diminishing sound of hoofbeats, taking Thomas so unexpectedly out of her life; her grandfather's change of heart which Doctor Marsh had thought would tie her against her inclination, but in fact would set her free.

Free. But to what purpose? She closed her eyes, seeing again the hurt on Adam's face, hearing the bitterness in his voice. By her own weakness and folly she had sent him from her. Would he ever forgive her? Was it too late?

The words 'too late' brought her up sharply. What was it Thomas had said, a few minutes ago?

'You had better look again—except that it might be too late.'

He had seemed so sure that he had a case against Adam. But how could he have? There was no real evidence, no possibility of contraband being found, according to Adam. Thomas's words repeated themselves in her mind. 'You had better look again . . . look again.'

She ran to the stables, calling to the garden-boy to saddle her pony.

'But I've only just ridden him to Honiton and back, ma'am,' he protested.

'Do as I say, and quickly,' she insisted.

While she waited impatiently, Paul came out of the house.

'Where are you going, Aunt Jocelyn?' he asked.

'To Galliards.'

He scuffed his toe against the cobbles. 'Martha says we may have to leave Penn Barton. Is that true?'

He was looking up at her with the same expression of anxiety she had seen on his face when he broke the news that he had brought his sisters from Plymouth. More than any words, his eyes told her that he was as afraid now as he had been then. There must seem to him no more security here, in the house in which his mother had lived, than anywhere else.

The garden-boy had his back towards them. There was no one else about. She put her arms around Paul and held him close.

'We are all staying at Penn Barton, darling, for as long as we wish. Only now, it will be different. We shall all be happy together, for we need no longer be afraid.'

For a moment he clung to her; then he drew away.

'I wasn't afraid of great-grandfather,' he declared stoutly. 'But I didn't want to be sent away and not know what was happening to my sisters.'

As the garden-boy held the pony for Jocelyn to mount, Paul asked, 'Are you going to see Captain Perevell?'

She paused with a foot in the stirrup. 'I—don't know, dear. I can only hope that I will.'

Cantering through the village, Jocelyn was conscious of the stir of curiosity which followed her progress. The sight of Miss Harmer of Penn Barton Manor, most unsuitably dressed and with her hair blowing in the breeze, riding post haste to the house of the Peverells on the day of her grandfather's funeral, would provide subject for gossip for weeks ahead.

Gravel spurted from the pony's hooves as she rode on to the terrace. A workman, carrying a load of bricks, came around a corner of the house. Startled, he dropped his load. The pony shied, almost unseating Jocelyn.

'Where is Captain Peverell?' she demanded.

The man scratched his head. 'Don't rightly know, ma'am.'

'You mean, he is not here?'

'That's right. He's not been here since early this morning.'

A second workman came along the terrace to join them. They were both strangers to Jocelyn.

'You looking for Captain Peverell, ma'am? If so, you'd best try down the combe. I caught sight of un a while since, making towards the beach.'

Jocelyn hesitated. She could guess Adam's reason for going towards the sea instead of returning to Galliards. On the cliff he could be alone. That was surely what he would want after her seeming rejection of him.

Her first impulse was to go to him, to beg his forgiveness and tell him that she was free. But she had ridden to Galliards for another purpose, which would not be served by seeking Adam on the cliffs.

Telling the men she would wait, she dismounted and tethered the pony. Then, with a casual air, she walked towards the group of outbuildings. At the entrance to the tumbledown barn she looked back. The two men had returned to their work. There was no one in sight.

She went into the barn and stood for a moment or two, accustoming her eyes to the dimness. At first glance, it seemed to her that nothing had changed. Then she looked more closely at the broken-down cart, and caught her breath. There was hay in it, fresh hay.

Cautiously she made her way over the uneven floor. Reaching the cart, she saw that the robin's nest was deserted, the eggs broken. She stepped up on to a wheel and pushed aside some of the hay. Underneath was a small barrel, of the type which contained spirits. Swiftly she pushed aside more hay. The cart was full of kegs.

Jocelyn climbed down off the wheel. She stood in the

dark barn, not knowing what to do. Someone had put the kegs there without Adam's knowledge, it was obvious. Someone who had doubtless been bribed to do so. By Thomas?

For the moment, neither the person responsible nor the method used, was important. It was imperative that Adam should be informed what had happened before the Preventive Officer came. She was quite sure that he would have been sent word that there was a chance of finding contraband at Galliards.

She started at the sound of a footfall outside. If it should be the Preventive Officer, what was she to say? He had already come upon her in Martha's cottage. If he should find her here, might not her presence do more harm than good to Adam?

She pressed herself against the wagon as the footsteps came nearer. Then, as a man's figure appeared in the doorway, she cried out in relief.

'Adam! Oh, thank heaven it is you!'

She ran forward and clutched at his arm. 'Listen. Please listen to me.'

He stood rigid, his face set.

He said coldly, 'I was under the impression there was nothing more to say.'

Involuntarily, at his tone, she stepped back.

He went on speaking.

'My men informed me that a lady who appeared in some distress was enquiring for me and had walked this way.' Suddenly his voice became angry and he pushed her aside.

'What have you been doing in here? What trick have you and that damned lawyer been playing to me?'

'There *has* been a trick,' she said. 'But I had no part in it, I swear!'

He was staring at the cart. Where she had moved the hay, a keg showed plainly. He turned and caught hold of her wrist so tightly that she cried out.

'I came to warn you,' she protested. 'Oh, it does not matter what you think of me. But save yourself. Get rid of those kegs before the Preventive Officer comes. Adam, I beg of you, do as I say.'

There was doubt in his eyes. He was silent for a few moments.

Then he said, 'I have just seen both Preventive Officers putting out to sea. There is a customs cutter lying off-shore. Doubtless they have gone to confer. There is no chance of their reaching here for some while.'

'Oh, thank heaven! Then you will have time.'

He released her wrist and stood back, regarding her from head to foot. He said reflectively. 'Your pony is lathered, and you are not wearing a riding habit or boots. Did you really ride here in such haste on my account?'

'Why else? If you were taken by the customs men and sent to prison . . .'

'It could scarcely affect you, Jocelyn. My life now is no concern of yours. Nor yours, apparently, of mine.'

She bent her head. 'That is for you to say.'

He stepped forward. 'What do you mean?'

'I am not to marry Thomas Creedy. Grandfather made a new will yesterday. He has left everything to Isabella and appointed me as her guardian. I have no dowry. Therefore Thomas Creedy does not want me any more.'

He gripped her shoulders. 'Are you telling me the truth—this time?'

She looked straight into his eyes. 'Yes. I am truly free now. But I do not suppose you will ever forgive me.' Her control broke and she had to fight back tears.

'You must believe I had no choice over the marriage,' she said desperately. 'Grandfather forced me into it just as he forced me to stay with him and to keep away from you. Adam, I know it was wrong not to tell you of my betrothal. But I wanted you to love me, I wanted a little happiness before I was condemned to a life of—of . . .'

She could no longer continue. She laid her head against his chest in a gesture of submission.

'I love you. I love you, Adam. Please forgive me.'

For a moment he made no move. Then his arms went around her and she was held close and safe.

He said tenderly, 'My poor darling. Don't cry, Jocelyn. There's no need for tears, my love. It's all over now, all the unhappiness. I'll take care of you—and the children.'

She raised her head. Even in the semi-darkness she could see the brightness of his eyes, the smiling curve of his lips. Joy surged through her whole being. She did not believe any woman had been loved with such selfless devotion. But now it was possible for her to return his love in full measure, to hold nothing back.

She flung her arms around his neck and laughed delightedly as he swung her off her feet and whirled her around in a wild, exultant dance. When he kissed her, the incongruous surroundings of the old, ruined barn faded away and she could have believed there was sunlight all about them, and the sound of the sea in their ears.

Rona Randall

45121	Knight's Keep	75c
54325	Mountain of Fear	75c
87100	Walk Into My Parlor	50c
89000	The Willow Herb	60c

Virginia Coffman

05271	The Beckoning	75c
14293	The Devil Vicar	75c
13791	The Dark Gondola	75c
52100	Masque by Gaslight	75c
86020	The Vampyre of Moura	75c

The Novels Of

Jane Blackmore

Just 75¢ Each

05551 Beware The Night

08010 Bridge Of Strange Music

08200 Broomstick In The Hall

14201 Deed Of Innocence

14208 The Deep Pool

53485 The Missing Hour

64281 The Other Mother

77905 Square Of Many Colours

78587 Stephanie

80827 Three Letters To Pan

86091 The Velvet Trap

90814 A Woman On Her Own

Available wherever paperbacks are sold or use this coupon.

BESTSELLERS!

THE ANCHORMAN by Ned Calmer. For the first time —the sensational novel of network news coverage and a top newscaster—his life, his passions, his conflicts, and his many loves. (02266—$1.50)

THE FACE OF THE THIRD REICH by Joachim Fest. Like the Speer memoirs . . . a detailed portrait of 18 Nazi leaders, brought to life as individuals. (22560—$1.95)

JUNKIE by William Burroughs. The classic drug novel of the "beat" generation, by the author of **NAKED LUNCH**. (41841—60c)

THE LEFT HAND OF DARKNESS by Ursula LeGuin. An award-winning science fiction novel of adventure on a planet where everyone is the same sex—a combination of mythology and psychology. (47800—95c)

"LONG AGO, TOMORROW" by Peter Marshall. A sensitive, touching, sometimes funny, sometimes sad love story. (48880—75c)

THE RED BARON by Manfred von Richthofen. The autobiography of the most famous air ace of World War I. (71000—75c)

THE SCALE WATCHER'S DIET by Evelyn Fiore. At last—a diet that's easy to live with. Try these delicious enticing recipes that count carbograms instead of calories. (75300—75c)

THE SHROUDED WALLS by Susan Howatch. Marianne Fleury married her husband for money . . . but things became complicated when she realized she loved him and he was accused of murder. By the author of the bestselling **PENMARRIC**. (76291—75c)

Available wherever paperbacks are sold or use this coupon.

ac€ **books,** (Dept. MM) Box 576, Times Square Station New York, N.Y. 10036

Please send me titles checked above.

I enclose $. . . . . Add 15¢ handling fee per copy.

Name . . . .

Address . . . .

City. State. . . . . Zip. . . . .

Please allow 4 weeks for delivery. 30A

Silhouette Romances

All titles priced at 75c.

34301	Hotel De Luxe	Rona Randall
76551	The Silver Cord	Rona Randall
14201	Deed of Innocence	Jane Blackmore
80827	Three Letters to Pan	Jane Blackmore
80530	That Night At the Villa	Sheila Bishop
14275	Desperate Decision	Sheila Bishop

Available wherever paperbacks are sold or use this coupon.

ace books, (Dept. MM) Box 576, Times Square Station
New York, N.Y. 10036
Please send me titles checked above.

I enclose $................Add 15¢ handling fee per copy.

Name ....

Address ....

City.................... State............ Zip........

Please allow 4 weeks for delivery.   39

The Gothic Mysteries Of

Margaret Erskine

Just 75¢ Each

09209	Caravan Of Night
09215	The Case Of Mary Fielding
14120	Dead By Now
15900	Don't Look Behind You
28940	Give Up The Ghost
30251	Graveyard Plot
64595	The Painted Mask
86602	Voice Of The House
86605	The Voice Of Murder

Available wherever paperbacks are sold or use this coupon.

ace books, (Dept. MM) Box 576, Times Square Station
New York. N.Y. 10036

Please send me titles checked above.

I enclose $.................Add 15¢ handling fee per copy.

Name ....

Address ....

City.................... State.............. Zip.........
Please allow 4 weeks for delivery.

Regency Romances by Elizabeth Renier and Sheila Bishop

17521	Durable Fire	Bishop	75c
22860	Favorite Sister	Bishop	75c
34410	House of Granite	Renier	75c
34454	House of Water	Renier	75c
36335	If This Be Love	Renier	75c
58355	No Hint of Scandal	Bishop	75c
65862	Penelope Devereux	Bishop	75c
80730	Tomorrow Comes the Sun Renier		75c
85910	Valley of Secrets	Renier	75c
90833	Woman from the Sea	Bishop	75c

There are a lot more
where this one came from!